QUEBEC

TIM CASTANO

QUEBEC

A NOVEL

LIBRARY OF CONGRESS CATALOGING-IN-PUBLICATION DATA
Quebec
Authored by Tim Castano
ISBN: 978-0-9994617-8-5
LCCN: 2019956451

FOR MOM AND DAD

Contents

1

MY MOTHER OFTEN TOLD THE STORY.

The account grew into familial mythology, much in the way most mythology imposes comforting contours around a universe, leaving the contents a little more orderly, a little less infinite.

Having reached her early forties, her three young children in school, supported fully by her husband, drowning in oceans of talent, my mother did not know what to do next with her life.

So, she took a trip to a familiar location.

She drove eight hours north—"wending my way," as she described it—the travel as therapeutic as the destination.

Outside of Quebec City, she visited the Basilica of Sainte-Anne-de-Beaupré to pray for guidance.

My mother returned home to learn she was several weeks pregnant.

In her mind, Saint Anne had given the answer.

2

"I FLEW UP TONIGHT … I didn't want to worry you … Quebec … It's in Canada … You have been here … Many times, I thought … I must be wrong, then … I will be home on Monday night, so I won't see you tomorrow … I will call tomorrow … I will … I do, too."

Iridescent yellow and red blurs streaked the taxi window. A Burger King. A McDonald's. Of course, several Tim Hortons. Flashes of the familiar and the pseudo-exotic. Enough of the same. Enough of the different. A picture of the safe escapism that draws some Americans to Canada: *Like home, but not quite.*

"Wife?" the driver asked.

"Mother."

"You still call your mother? Good son. How old are you? Thirty? Thirty-one?"

"A few years older than that."

"It's time for you to get a wife to call."

"We'll see."

"I had both once. Now, neither. My mother died. Cancer. My wife, she lives with another man now, back in Syria."

He did not hesitate, so eager to unburden himself. Perhaps he could have had any number of jobs, but driving a cab supplied him with a steady rotation of captive audiences. He could share his history with a stranger late on a Saturday evening in October. If this were the outlet he desired, not much could compete with such a perk.

"I'm sorry to hear that."

"I'm sorry, too. I ride this thing around to send her money, but she doesn't need it. The new man has plenty. That's why she left me for him."

My few-months-younger self would have referenced my own situation. During an earlier phase, I would have introduced the topic to almost anyone. Friends. Casual acquaintances. Retail personnel. Show me the slightest crack and I would have jammed in the conversational crowbar. I eventually realized how I had made others uncomfortable, as uncomfortable as I felt in that taxi, shifting a bit in my seat, my molars grinding away at the memories. Back then—not so long ago, really—I had no idea what I hoped to hear. Now on the other side, I understood those with whom I had spoken also had no idea what to say. They were patient, though, and kind and gracious, remarkably so. I wish I could apologize to each of them. I suppose among the indulgences one could sample under the circumstances—getting a profane tattoo, joining a cult—talking a little too much is excusable. Still, if I could have counseled my earlier self, I would have advised: "Keep quiet."

In that cab, I obeyed. I chose silence. I could have changed the subject—"Did you know Ronnie Garvin is from Quebec?"—or offered some vending-machine maxim—"Life has a way of working out"—not dissimilar from what some might have said to me in the recent past. Instead, I hoped enough wordless seconds had elapsed for the driver and I to agree our discussion had ended.

The car accelerated, as if to message: *No need for talk, then no reason for delay.* The pieces of a city began to assemble, the outskirts dotted with thickening clumps of large, angular structures, all steel and glass. Then, we reached Rue Saint Louis. Modern materials gave way to stone and brick. Cosmopolitan utility bowed to the bygone charm of dormers, awnings, hanging signs, flower boxes.

Arriving at night in a town you do not know can intoxicate, as if you could wobble around and trip over a rock, hitting the ground with a laugh or a curse, depending on your state of mind. Quebec in darkness left me with the sense I could fall off a steep cliff with one wrong step, plunging down until flailing awake in my bed, the visit just a dream. I opened the window a little. The air widened my eyes, but the late hour hid the very reason why I had traveled there. I could have kept closer to home to see streetlamps and four-story-high buildings.

The taxi did not slow as the road narrowed. Without even tapping the break, the driver jerked the steering wheel a sharp left, then a sharper left in what seemed like an illegal turn down an alley not intended for vehicles. He stopped.

"There you go. Hotel Sainte Anne." He sounded bitter we had not become better acquainted during the ride.

The driver pulled away before the door even fully closed. Had he deposited me at the wrong address, I would have a problem. No one could point me in the correct direction. Even if I called out for help, I would have heard only the echo of my voice in the eerie emptiness, as if a neutron bomb had cleared the region of all human beings. Walking into the hotel lobby, no one greeted me, just as the woman on the phone had noted when I made the reservation that morning. I found an envelope with my name, the key inside.

My room wore such a deliberate style, perhaps what a high-priced decorator might categorize as "authentic minimalism," a euphemism for "less expensive than the Chateau Frontenac." I could imagine the same decorator accentuating the exposed brick wall and insisting on the chestnut-finished built-ins, the gray subway-tiled bathroom with its basin sink and counterintuitive-counterclockwise faucet fixture. A small writing desk completed the contemporary monasticism. It suited me.

I hoped I would fall asleep quickly. More importantly, I hoped I would stay asleep. For too many months, I would drift off with ease, then open my eyes only twenty minutes later, refreshed enough for hours and hours of relentless second-guessing and obsessive projection. If I could cure any tendency, I would rid myself of disjointed sleep, just for a few days during a week.

In the bed, I turned over on my stomach, face pressed sideways on the mattress, the pillow over my head, my preferred position. I breathed deeply and said out loud, "Here I am."

3

I WAS CALM.

When I think of the day my divorce proceeded—an experience that crosses my mind less and less over time—I remember I was calm. I have heard of individuals whose lives had swerved in a single episode—an accident, an illness, a defeat—who met the decisive instant with poise. If not poise, an absence of mania. Catastrophe, I always had feared, would wring from me some mixture of hysteria and apoplexy. When my teetering marriage suddenly, finally and irretrievably fell on the side of dissolution, I took some solace in the fact I was calm.

Relatively so. At least to me.

To those I engaged during the first days and months, I sputtered like an electrical appliance dropped in a full tub: shocked useless, the remnants of once-functional components inside a charred shell. Those who knew me well understood. They understood how only a few weeks earlier, I would have stated with unending confidence that I enjoyed the happiest of marriages. They understood the enormity of my filing for divorce.

When I exited my house on what I would have to describe as a bad morning, I was obsessed with the "why" and the "how," of course. But my mind immediately, oddly turned to a more insignificant concern: *I will have to come up with my answer.* Any time the topic of marriage would surface in the future, instead of citing the number of years together or giving the quick version of how it began, I would have to give the quick version of how it had ended. If I had listened more closely over the years, perhaps I would have heard the wisdom already earned by those who, themselves, had endured bad mornings.

"It just did not work out. I'm in a better place."

"We wanted different things. I wish him the best."

"We were young. We changed. We're still friends."

I likely had dismissed these statements as curt haikus of regret and denial, throwaway lines written for strangers at events to bring a fast close to an uncomfortable discussion. The authors had vacuumed it up, sealed it shut in a tight, tidy package. To reduce a marriage— the beginning, the middle and, most importantly, the end—simply to "it" demonstrates the method's effectiveness. I perhaps had attributed the approach to discretion or self-protection. At my worst—at my most judgmental—I possibly had attributed the approach to intellectual and emotional laziness.

I was wrong. As I have learned, these individuals painstakingly and painfully had chiseled down confusion, self-recrimination, concession and acceptance into those few phrases. This editorial process, I unwittingly had entered on that first day. A vexing, frustrating process of word choice and argument and positioning.

Instinctively, you wish to shape the narrative. Even as information gushes freely and without form, you steer the flow in certain directions. You soon recognize the fewer details you offer, the more room you allow for another person to speculate. Even a benign, blanket remark—"I was not perfect"—carves out such a wide berth. For example, on one end of the grievance spectrum, the purchase of the wrong flowers on the sixth anniversary of the third date could represent imperfection. On the other end, you might have fathered a secret second family in Argentina. The less you say, the more some all-too willingly comment for you and about you. The more you say, the greater the risk of ugliness on your part. You cannot help but feel defenseless and defensive at almost every turn.

Family and friends had cautioned me not to care what others might have thought. I did care, though, because I am human or, more precisely, a certain type of human. Family and friends also had predicted I ultimately would not concern myself with the "why" and the "how." Right on both counts, they were, as usual. It just took time for them to be right. More time than I would have hoped. Eventually, I became tired of the explanations. My story began to bore me, the monotonous this-and-then-that progression. Fatigue, not a breakthrough, prompted the slicing and splicing and consolidation. I shortened my account. Shortened it again. Added some perspective. Then, one day, someone inquired about my marriage and I said: "My wife fell in love with someone else. I'm not exactly certain when she fell out of love with me."

I would have to live with that answer. I had no choice.

On that initial morning, I left my house with many days ahead of me before I would reach those sentences. But I was calm. And alert, purposefully so. I tried to hover above myself with mindful recitation, a practice I never before had undertaken: *My hands are on the steering wheel. The sun is shining across the windshield. I am driving.* The breeze and heat through the open windows interrupted my interior monologue to confirm, *Yes, this is happening.* I recorded details: the black paint on the fire hydrants, the speed of the vehicles around me, the number of branches on the tree near a traffic light. My environment seemed different, so it also must look different, I reasoned. No. The world was the same. I, the receptor, had changed. I was skin scraped raw after falling off a bicycle, cringing and sore when first touched by sweat and Bactine.

Even fully stationary, sitting still in the vehicle, I felt myself floating into uncertain space. I called a friend and asked if I could visit him at work, a perhaps out-of-bounds request to many, but not to him. We walked around the paths near his building for a few minutes. I observed the slow-motion formation of disbelief in the furrowed brow and dilated pupils and subtle drop of the chin, as if I told him I had been in a major accident. A quick, destructive smash without precursor, yet with a lengthy recovery. Accident also as mistake, in that the development upended order and expectation so categorically as to suggest a cosmic clerical error.

A transcript of the conversation with my friend could have passed for a Rorschach test. I splattered ink into the atmosphere, with no regard for continuity or sense. I had to expel raw information, having yet to refine the situation in my own head. My friend was patient, as he would be throughout the ordeal. He asked the perfect proportion of questions: just enough to convey genuine concern, but not too many to discomfort me. I strained to strike an upbeat tone, conspicuously so. He focused on the positive: "You have a fantastic family, so many friends who love you. You're going to be great." We both knew the truth: This would be tough.

I returned to my car, to a phone with missed calls and messages from family members, the news pinging only among them. I spoke with each person. The word accident again captured the mood, with everyone—rattled, but assured—ticking through items on a post-disaster protocol: Safe? Stable? Mobile? Fed? I hurried through the exchanges, as if a long list of responsibilities begged for my attention. Quite the opposite, in fact.

I received one work-related call. I said to the person on the other end of the line, "I'm sorry I cannot talk right now," followed by a matter-of-fact explanation of the day's events. He laughed. After a prolonged pause, he stammered from incredulity—"You're kidding?"—to inquiry—"What happened?"—then landed on apology—"I'm so sorry." I had to come up with a more polished way to inform people.

I drove and drove, circling a practical challenge I would face almost every day during the upcoming months: I did not know where to go. I could not return to my home just then. My wife had chosen to leave and wanted time to remove some of her belongings. I did not trust myself in an open public setting, not confident in how I might react if I encountered someone I recognized. Irrationality barred me inside the car, as it would my house in the weeks ahead. I finally stopped across the street from a park. Through the driver's side window, I stared at an empty bench on the bank of a brook. I imagined myself sitting there in the shade, peacefully occupied by ordinary concerns, like having to clean out a garage or having to buy a greeting card. In my mind, the unknown becomes a blank, endless scroll on which to scribble disaster. So much was unknown right then. The blankest, most endless scroll had unfurled before me. I envied those with ordinary concerns. I wondered if I ever again would be a person in a park, worrying about having to clean out a garage or buy a greeting card.

I waited in that spot for such a duration, the local police justifiably could have tapped on my window and subjected me to light interrogation.

"May I ask what you are doing here, sir?"

"My marriage just ended this morning, so I thought I would stare at that empty bench."

"I'm going to have to ask you to get out of the car, sir."

Before a member of the law-enforcement community could list me in a database from which I could not be expunged, the time had come to head to the bookstore coffee shop where my father and I had agreed to meet when we spoke earlier in the day. Neither of us knew exactly what we intended to achieve when we set the appointment, but it felt like a natural enough response. I waited in the bookstore's lot only a few minutes before he appeared. We each climbed out of our cars and approached one another slowly, hauling the weight of expectations along with us. Our heads sloped downward, our eyes not quite ready to meet, we both attempted to organize our faces into impassive expressions. He wanted to show me my father would be no different. I wanted to show him his son would be no different. We also both had rehearsed what we would say to one other.

When I got to him, I asked, "How has your day been, Dad?"

He laughed and told me the name of someone who had withstood similar circumstances, only to have emerged with a seemingly improved lot. I imagined my father that afternoon thumbing through the frayed-edge cards of his gray-metal, mental rolodex—*Whom do I know who thrived after a divorce?*—searching for the example that just might break through my sadness. I loved him for the effort and, of course, so much more.

At the coffee shop, I ordered an orange soda, a strange choice, since I do not believe I had drunk orange soda since Sunkist had appropriated a song by the Beach Boys decades earlier. So much of the day already so abnormal, why not fill my empty stomach with fluorescent, carbonated syrup? My father selected iced tea. Our beverages I remember more clearly than I do much of our dialogue as we sat and talked, but I never will forget the two sensations that overcame me, the two sensations that would govern my foreseeable future: gratitude and guilt.

"A boy needs his father," one often hears. I would amend the statement to add, "So does a man." Modest, modern rites of passage, like playing catch or tying a tie, disclose to a boy when he needs his father. A man, though, may not understand when and how much until the moment arises, usually one of turbulence and uncertainty. I needed my father right then. I was profoundly grateful to have him. This singular perception would have to adjust my outlook moving forward: less fixated on what I had lost, more focused on all I retained.

The guilt bubbled up in the long pauses. We struggled with what to say to one another. Not a push-and-pull talk. More like passengers on a raft, drifting down a river, commenting on the surroundings.

"I didn't see this coming."

"Neither did I."

"You both seemed so happy."

"I thought we were, too."

"I just don't understand."

"Neither do I."

My father's sentences ached a little, caught in a section of his throat through which words usually glided. In the ellipses, in the verbal lurches, I noticed how much this hurt him, how he had to cast his look beyond me, not on me. I never before had recognized the pain a divorce visits upon those close to the two spouses. The in-laws who have come to love one another. The nieces and nephews who no longer would see an uncle or an aunt.

"I'm sorry, Dad."

"Nothing for you to be sorry about."

He waved off my concern, selflessly locking the attention on me. My guilt, though, would persist. Guilt for the sorrow I had delivered to him, particularly at a point when he deserved relief, not another complication.

The bookstore windows tinted darker and darker as the sun set, signaling I finally could return to my house. My father and I said goodbye to one another with some apprehension. Neither of us knew what to expect in the coming weeks, only that the subject and pattern of our conversations would stay rather stagnant. We would discuss little else other than my divorce for quite a while. Not sports or current events or family business. I already missed it.

Again behind the wheel of the car, windows open, the warm summer night coated my face, filled my chest. Never had I expected to have such an evening, a cluster of hours so vivid and consequential in how they went by, dividing all that came before from all that would follow. No grief in that trip home. Just ownership. It all would be mine, like it or not. The hurt. The frustration. The recovery. All of it would be my life.

I had silenced the radio during the day, foolishly angry at music, at the audacity of songwriters for even attempting to reflect or touch my situation. In the lulling smoothness of that brief drive, I pressed the "on" button and caught the drowsy piano stroll at the opening of "Bring It on Home to Me." Sam Cooke and Lou Rawls blended together their anguish, each "yeah" in their call-and-response convincing me: *I'm going to be all right.* Having made it to my driveway, I waited for the two to finish, as if they had performed only for me.

I walked into the house a bit uneasy. Had my wife left a note? She did not, which I appreciated. I could not have handled reading it. Would there be any apparent alterations? None jumped out at me, again gratefully so, as enough already had shifted in such a short period. I sat on the couch in the living room and listened to the quiet. The low, steady hum resounded with an endless quality, one with no threat of interruption, unnervingly so. I called a few close friends. I already had started to polish up the story. The facts, clearer. The sequence, tighter.

Then, I finally could conclude a day that began as a bad morning. Upstairs, I collapsed into a bed I had all to myself, yet I remained only on the side I had chosen, for no particular reason, nine years earlier. I knew only that I was at the beginning.

I was calm.

4

STEPPING OUT OF THE HOTEL Sainte Anne into that Sunday morning lifted the sheet covering a perfect display. Any nighttime ambivalence toward the city dropped into the Saint Lawrence River. I almost could taste the colors, the streams of gold sunlight and the crisp, warm flavor of auburn running down my throat like cider and syrup. Too small for the full, pure chill I inhaled, my lungs hurt with the gratitude of muscles pushed to their limits. Walking around the courtyard felt like a long recess in grade school. The nods and smiles among early-rising strangers—armed with coffee cups and cameras and folded maps—gestured our communal appreciation for the architects and planners and landscapers and, of course, for nature itself.

Perhaps for the rest of my days, when I think of an ideal form of autumn, I will remember that morning. I leaned over the railing at the Terrasse Dufferin, looking down on the Old City and toward the docked cruise ships. I continued to the end of the Terrasse and tried to see even just the edge of the Plains of Abraham. I sill do not know what I managed to catch, but it was green and lush and flat. Then, I became anxious, as I often do.

I could miss something. Allowing impulse to lead you around a foreign city appeals to romantic, not practical sensibilities. My schedule did not leave enough time for the romantic. I could hear someone asking when I returned home, "Did you see the 'blank'?" That I had not seen the "blank" would have downgraded the visit. I had to prioritize.

One "blank," I could not miss, the very reason for the trip.

Only a few doors from the Hotel Sainte Anne stood the Centre Infotouriste de Quebec, with its ale-foam walls, rows of green-rimmed windows and gray trim. I could envision a mass-produced miniature model of the building hunted by collectors desperate to complete their holiday villages. I came to a single, strong conclusion as soon as I walked in: *I would like to work here.* The vibe struck a balance between suspended reality and functionality. Yes, the operation primarily dispatched tourists on idyllic romps of sightseeing and eating and drinking, but those tourists would know exactly where to go and feel confident heading there, thanks to the bubbly sentinels stationed behind the counters. Theirs seemed a happy vocation, which I envied.

"Parlez-vous anglais?"

I lathered the mangled syllables with enough earnestness the gentleman would have had to pity me with

English. At the very least, he would have wished to spare himself another assault on the French language.

"Welcome to Quebec. How might I help you?"

Late-fifties with the energy of a workshop elf, he sported a beard I immediately respected, one worn unfashionably for decades, surviving long enough to live peacefully in an era that exalts facial hair. He also so obviously would not have resembled the same person without the beard, as if the Abominable Snowman were shaved down to reveal an accountant. I indicated where I wished to visit and inquired about renting a vehicle for the day.

"You could get a car, but I would suggest one of the tours. Much cheaper and more to see."

The word "tour" evoked scenes of infantilizing guides with megaphones and triangle flags, shepherding seniors into a series of gift shops. Even with my bias, I agreed. I did not want to let this man down. He appeared to exact a portion of his self-worth from having others follow his recommendations.

"You're in luck. There is room on the next bus. It leaves in seven minutes, right outside."

Seven minutes provided enough time for regret to bake, but not enough to remove it from the oven. An amoeba-like crowd formed in a general area of the courtyard. Whispers of uncertainty murmured among them. ("Is this where he said to wait?" "All of us for the same one?") Eventually and organically, the group arranged itself in a straight line. I latched on at the tail.

Those gathered studied one another as strangers do at the start of an artificial, five-hour relationship: pretending to gaze into the distance when actually swiping fast glimpses of the person in front of you, behind you. As expected, I was the only one alone.

I had learned to accept the suspiciousness of a man my age on his own. A solitary male traveler in his late-thirties invites others to write his story more so than read it. I almost could hear the traditionally minded stacking up their adjectives: reckless, promiscuous, transgressive. The more forgiving would use gentler, yet still loaded descriptors: unfinished, indecisive, lost. Some would wonder: *What did he do wrong?* With a touch of jealousy, others would wonder: *What did he do right?*

Of course, the truth spanned between mildly interesting and unbearably boring, no doubt a disappointment to all of them. I have experienced this suspicion as inconvenience. The prior night, upon arrival at the airport, the immigration agent ushered me to a side room for an interview. She scrutinized each page of the passport with an intensity that piqued my own curiosity.

"You've been here before?" she asked firmly, without eye contact.

"No."

"Your passport says you were in Canada several years ago, no?" She arched her left eyebrow, the first sign of an actual human characteristic. Her platinum hair pulled back severely in a bun, her cheekbones knife-edge sharp, her skin without a line, she might have been a prototype from the robotics division of a technology firm.

"I thought you meant Quebec. Yes, I have been to Canada."

"It looks as if you booked your flight only this morning. Why?"

"My other plans fell through at the last minute."

This was a lie. I had no other plans. I considered lightening the mood by saying, "What is the point of being able to go somewhere whenever you want unless you actually do it?" I judged the comment a tad too flippant, perhaps handing her the excuse she needed to remand me to a cell.

"Welcome to Canada," she said, returning my passport as if it were a red-marked test on which I had scored only a single point above failure.

I got on the tour bus, observed as an oddity by those already assembled. On one side of the aisle, a family of five with preemptively bored teenagers. On the other, a family of four with two children under ten, all of whom soon would discover the error in how they chose to spend their day. A few younger-to-middle-aged couples on fall getaways. The rest of the bus carted likely retirees in their sixties and seventies. After taking me in, some tilted their heads a few degrees to the right or the left, hopeful to see a trailing companion, a person who might have had to use the restroom or had forgotten an item at the hotel.

I sat in the last row, slid down against the pleather cushions and put in my headphones. I scrolled through my six-hundred-and-seven songs. The number marked both an accomplishment and an embarrassment. I had begun with the sum of almost all beginnings: zero. I had built my collection one-by-one, each privately enlarging my sense of personal autonomy. (Yes, I understood I lugged around an auditory metaphor.) For ninety-nine cents or one dollar and twenty-nine cents, I could buy a few minutes of poignancy, transport, perspective, uplift, commiseration, defiance, acceptance, resilience, fun. I rationalized the habit as cheap and, when compared to other diversions, harmless. Soon the habit became unwieldy and, in the aggregate, somewhat expensive. The scope partly owed to my no-judgment policy. If I enjoyed a song, I would download it. Perhaps a forgotten B-side track. Maybe a childhood memory spun off my oldest brother's turntable, with those inscrutable lyrics that had promised to explain themselves when I reached adolescence. Or the latest release from a breakout artist, a practice that maintained my fraying connection to the modern world and reminded me how much unrecorded music awaits us. (Again, metaphor.) Some mornings, I would awake a bit foggy and ask: *Did I really buy that?* Newly single men, I suspect, can start days with bigger regrets.

I wish I could review a chart that displayed the date and time when I had listened to a particular song. The selections would say more about me at a specific point than I ever could communicate. I would hear those dawn-darkness rides on sleepy trains, when I could not conceive of trudging through the upcoming hours. (Marvin Gaye's "Trouble Man" or Crowded House's "Pour le monde.") I would hear those afternoons I had to close my office door, because I no longer could interact with another human being. (Elvis Costello's "Man Out of Time" or Duke Ellington's "In My Solitude.") I would hear the long, mind-clearing Saturday slogs through the reservation. (The Head and the Heart's "Another Story" or Brandi Carlile's "That Wasn't Me.") I would hear the evenings alone in my house, needing a summation of that day and a reason to expect the next one could improve. (The Five Stairsteps' "O-O-H Child" or Johnnie Taylor's "I Believe in You.")

Often, I would choose music incongruous with the moment, as I did on the bus as it maneuvered its way out of the city: Earth, Wind and Fire's "Let's Groove." I cannot recall many occasions when I would not welcome "Let's Groove." Winding down the sloping streets, the driver stopped at two hotels farther out to retrieve more passengers. A number of them boarded with a crabby, what-took-you-so-long irritation. I raised the volume, never more grateful for Maurice White and Philip Bailey's vocals.

5

I DID NOT KNOW IF MY MOTHER WOULD UNDERSTAND.
I suspect many children worry how parents will respond to a divorce. A father might express disappointment. A mother, heartbreak. Cultural mores bruised. Religious norms bashed. Relatives might conduct a quick history lesson to underscore your pioneer status: "No one in the family ever has gotten divorced." They might go so far as to implicate you in involuntary manslaughter: "My friend's son got divorced and it killed his father." In addition to having suffered an intensely personal fracture, to some, you suddenly carry a communicable disease.

My concern with sharing the news with my mother reached a level more fundamental than possible melodrama. I did not know if she would understand divorce as a concept.

Around four years earlier, my family began to detect the signs. Even in your speech, you bracket "the signs" in quotations marks. At first, she struggled with the names of those she knew quite well, even her children and grandchildren.

"Of course I know who you are. You just look different today."

Then, descriptions overtook names.

"We went to that place on the avenue, across from that big church. You know the one I'm talking about."

"Those people came over. You know, the nice guy and his wife and his daughters."

Just natural stumbles on the treadmill of advancing age, our best-case-scenario selves would rationalize. We would reference those relatives whose mental acuity had dulled a bit at the edges without softening fully into debilitation. The euphemism "forgetfulness" darkened when we would dine in restaurants and my mother would not bother with the menu, but would say, "You know what I like. Why don't you order for me?" She could read, but she could not recall the association between the word and the item. She also could not remember what food she actually enjoyed.

"This is so good. I've never eaten anything like this before."

She had, as recently as the previous day.

Dialogue traveled in circuits, the subjects kept within the safe confines of generalities. She also relied increasingly on conversational crutches to steady herself.

"That's life, right? What are you going to do?"

From time to time, she could dazzle with lucidity. She would bump into a person whom she had not seen in many years and call her by name without a beat. Or she would remind us of a minor, lost incident from our family's past. The very fact lucidity prompted surprise should have sounded alarms, but we permitted optimism and fear to deafen us. Then, we would catch her bewildered with the microwave oven or the television remote control, completely unaware of the function. The lucidity just smoke and sparks from a cruel magic trick.

Only when looking backward could we map—and fathom—her decline. We would remember tasks she had completed nine or ten months earlier, like dialing the telephone, all suddenly beyond her capabilities. She would settle on a plateau for a period, until dropping down and farther down. Her mind did not slip casually into dormancy. No, her mind worked like crazy to compensate, clawing to remain on whatever plain it inhabited. Such an agonizing distance between her and the world during that phase. A fight she waged silently by herself, for herself.

Eventually, less and less for her to grab and hold. Just deletion.

"I never knew you had a sister," she screamed at my father. "You never told me. Why am I finding this out now?"

My mother and my father's sister—my aunt—had known one another for over fifty years.

We, of course, had discussed my mother's condition as a family. An observation—"She is collecting spoons"—or an unfortunate event—locking herself out of the house when retrieving the mail—would trigger individual, one-off exchanges that became group email chains, then face-to-face meetings. We consulted physicians, surreptitiously so, given her ferocious reluctance to address the matter. My brothers would take her for evaluations under different guises. ("I want you to meet my friend." "I am having some issues and would like you to be there with me.") We enlisted a memory-care specialist to outline how we might prepare for what awaited us. We sat around conference tables, each of us an adult professional, virtually helpless. I had drawn only one conclusion: This disease is a leviathan.

As she regressed, we had cabined her off from certain stresses, such as health scares within the family or career setbacks. We did so to limit her anxiety and, quite honestly, our own. She no longer possessed the context one acquires during a lifetime, the many examples of challenges faced and overcome that forge into perspective and personal philosophy. Courage, as much as any quality, had underpinned my mother's character. No individual intimidated her. No scenario frightened her. To see this once-intrepid personality become too afraid to step outside her own home dismayed all who knew her. We would reason with her, provide rock-solid assurances, but the faulty machinery of her consciousness ground any such comfort into powder. Enough of my mother, though, still survived to notice I no longer would have a wife. I would have to tell her.

On a Saturday morning, just days after the divorce had been set in motion, my three brothers and I arranged to visit my parents and explain to my mother what had occurred. We each drove up to the house simultaneously, an unusual demonstration of organizational precision. Men have a way of speaking when they are expected to talk like men. Short, generic sentences, like among a group of football coaches.

"Gentlemen."

"How is everyone this morning?"

"Let's do this."

At the door of my childhood home, my mother welcomed us with a joy unspoiled by questions over why we were there or why we had shown up at the exact same time. She had become more suspicious where she should have been less and less suspicious where she should have been more. When you see a person with some frequency, you do not necessarily record the changes in appearance, the subtle, pixel-by-pixel modifications that accumulate into an older face, an aged body. I deliberately paid attention to her right then. She did not look almost-eighty, something immutably youthful in her eyes, in her features. Always sturdy, her frame had become more slender. In some ways, she seemed healthier than in the past, having lost some weight around her cheeks, through her middle. But she very much hovered on the border between fit and sickly, soon to cross over completely into the latter.

My brothers executed the perfect opening act as we gathered in the living room. They led a genial back-and-forth—"The kids said to say hello"—easing my mother into the best of moods and gently dropping the conversation on the spot where I would have to pick it up. Never had I felt quite as much like an adult, in the worst of ways. In general, I felt more like an adult getting divorced than I did when getting married. Marriage seemed like a way to preserve innocence, while divorce seemed like spending all day in a casino that does not comply with the health code.

"Mom, there is a reason we all are here right now. Everyone and everything is fine, but I need to tell you something."

I attempted to hold my voice as steady as possible. I worried even a slight tremble could set off an emotional chain reaction. She could have panicked, which would have toppled my shaky composure. Or she might have shot off impertinent questions, which I would have answered counterproductively. An outburst sat inside me, I knew. One I had neutralized, but I could do so for only so long.

To her extreme credit, my mother did not react on that Saturday morning. As I detailed the situation, I wondered how she pieced together the facts, if she could follow the trail of information to its definitive conclusion. She certainly appeared to grasp the seriousness. She maintained strong, firm eye contact. She did not interrupt. When I finished, she said in a dignified, graceful tone, "Okay."

That one word, as well as how she spoke it, relaxed me, the space between my eyes, at the base of my forehead, opening like a clamped hand. My mother rose to the occasion. I believe she did so for my benefit. She had buried her pain and confusion, the illness having yet to corrupt her maternal instinct.

Her brain then staggered its way through my story. She repeated certain lines, although packaged as inquiries. ("What you are saying is …") She struggled with some of the points, especially the speed with which everything had unraveled. She could not quite accept the permanence of the decision. In fairness, even at her sharpest, she might have resisted the finality, the closing of a door once and for all. My brothers and father swooped in with reinforcement.

"He is doing great."

"He will be more than fine."

We extended the discussion perhaps beyond necessity, returning again and again to the headline, our volume and confidence underscoring the key facts in bold. We had ensnared ourselves in a verbal cycle from which we could not exit, perhaps an inherently masculine flaw. My mother, even somewhat hobbled, led us out to the conversation's conclusion.

"Well, I love you more than anything. We will get you through this. You will have whatever you need from us."

We each stood and stretched and exhaled, all a bit in slow motion. My brothers talked of their rather normal plans for the day in rather normal tones, a warm-water reminder of the continuity in our lives, despite the jar and jerk of the divorce. My mother needed to hear how the everyday went on beyond that living room. So did I.

"I've got to take the kids to a practice, then we have a birthday party tonight."

"We want to get started on some planting for the front yard, so we're heading over to the garden store."

After they departed, I stayed behind with my parents for about two hours. I sank into the couch, into the feeling of home as much as the physical space. I returned in my mind to those Saturdays when much younger, maybe ten or eleven. My brothers out doing what older brothers do on weekends. Just my mother, father and I together for the evening. Mass, dinner, perhaps a trip to the video store. I was happy on those nights, even then aware it would not always last, that I would break off on my own, as all children do. Here we were years later, the three of us. Another Saturday. The questions before us weightier than what movie we would select.

I could have fallen asleep right then—for the first time in weeks, peacefully so. I continued talking, as if I had suffered a concussion and had to keep myself awake. I could neither ignore entirely the subject of the day, nor could I directly acknowledge it. Instead, I walked around the topic, as if surveying the damage from a car wreck.

"I still have no appetite. I don't think I've eaten for three days."

"My friends have called to check on me each day. Everyone has been really attentive."

My father asked questions that did not ignore entirely the subject, nor directly acknowledge it.

"How has it been living in the house?"

My mother was quiet. Selfishly, I would have described her as contemplative, because a more accurate word—withdrawn—carried heavier freight than I could manage right then. As my father and I spoke, she could not keep up with the fast transitions, like a runner still tying her sneakers long after the starter pistol had fired. All so unfair to her, as if we had spelled out strict terms: "We will discuss this seriously. Now, we will do so humorously. You can laugh here. Sorry, but you cannot raise a question there." Too much to ask of her. A naturally joyful person, she ordinarily would have overcompensated with chipper pronouncements. Not then. Just withdrawn. If angry about falling behind—her fear and insecurity sometimes exploded into anger—she did not betray it. Again, her maternal instinct prevailed, perhaps suppressing her own concerns for my sake.

"I think I'll head out now," I said.

"Why don't you stay here?" my mother asked.

I explained the reasons for my exit, all logical: tired, too much to do, etc. My mother invoked her own primal logic: *My son is hurt, so I want him close, to take care of him.* That I believed I could enter into an argument with her highlighted how vastly I misunderstood her condition. I obstinately would re-learn this lesson over and over. I just hugged her and made my way to the car. I drew temporary relief from the image of her standing on the front steps, waving at me as I drove off.

Everything had unfolded better than I had feared. At least she had allowed me to think as much. Later that evening, when I called my parents, my father said that after my departure, my mother hurled at him question after question: How could this have occurred? When did he know? What would happen next?

"Is she mad at me?"

"Not at you. At me."

"I'm sorry, Dad."

"Nothing for you to be sorry about."

"Does she understand?"

"Yes and no."

"That makes two of us."

6

ACCORDING TO MY MOTHER, centuries ago, fishermen from Canada sailed into an unforgiving tempest. Lost at sea, they prayed to Saint Anne for deliverance. She answered. The weather suddenly quieted and the fisherman returned home. They honored Saint Anne with the construction of a chapel that ultimately became the shrine standing today.

I had researched the history of Sainte-Anne-de-Beaupré before my flight to Quebec. I had found in certain sources enough traces of my mother's account to confirm it. I was, in all honesty, somewhat surprised. Facts and truth had not always aligned in her worldview. She respected facts. She had labored in them as a newspaper reporter and editor. As a playwright and creative writer, though, she required greater license in pursuit of the truth. Equilibrium likely existed between the two during a period in her life, but she eventually tipped in one's favor over the other. Facts could be adjusted in service of the truth. Embellishment anchored just enough in accuracy. Reductionism that preserved the bare minimum of detail.

We all do it. We also have it done to us, sometimes viciously so. With my mother, not a malicious tendency, but concurrently aggravating and beautiful. She could stretch thin, flimsy notions across a full canvas. She could lop off reason and relevance to fit within borders. In a way, she composed poetry. Certain verses maddening, others inspiring. Poetry, nonetheless.

Several facts surrounded Sainte-Anne-de-Beaupré: the donation of the land by a settler, the cured ailment of an original construction worker, the early-twentieth-century destruction by a fire. These points held far less value for my mother than the most poetic truth: A sacred place erected by those once adrift in an actual storm for later generations adrift in proverbial storms. The pithiness worked for her. I hoped it also might work for me.

Background on Sainte-Anne-de-Beaupré, I could find in a book. Some facts—truly important ones—forever would escape me.

I did not know why my mother first traveled to Quebec.

This realization snuck up on me during the second stop of the bus tour: a candy shop that peddled quaintness over quality. Glossy, brick-red paint and knobbed-wood shelves stocked with rows of clear-wrapped confections in the shape of maple leaves. My fellow passengers could have bought the same items in or near their hotels, but a store that resembled a cottage inhabited by friendly anthropomorphic forest animals persuaded them to load up on site.

In the candy shop, debating with myself over the purchase of gummy cola bottles, I wondered if one of my mother's many visits ever had detoured to such a place. Maybe on her maiden voyage, a mistake of the uninitiated. But I knew nothing about that first trip, in particular her motivation. I understood why she had returned on subsequent occasions. The initial one … Why? Had a family member or friend suggested it? Had she happened upon Sainte-Anne-de-Beaupré by accident? Had her interest developed in school, perhaps through one of those life-of-a-saint biographies a teacher sticks on a syllabus?

The reason remained a mystery. It always would, now encased in plaque, trapped by atrophy. I never had thought to ask my mother about the origins of her life-long dedication, the influences that had pointed her toward Quebec. Even during an earlier stage of her disease, when she could call up decades-old events with far greater clarity than she could the beginning of the very conversation in which she engaged, I had failed to appreciate the urgency. Did her memories recede like a tide, less and less of her with each weakening lap? Or erased as if by a quick tap on a keypad? Could I have asked her about Quebec on a Wednesday and received an answer? Had I waited until Thursday, would she have forgotten? Regardless, it was too late.

I walked back to the bus, the drag of gravity on my face, down to feet that scraped across the pebbles and dirt. You can bury yourself in the "dealing with it."

The concern for a person can break into constituent pieces—feeding, clothing, medicating—so much so you overlook the totality of the illness. Perhaps you force yourself to overlook, until halted still for a few seconds by a stealthy reminder. The reality of power-lessness and degradation a clenched fist around your heart. A reality you cannot ignore or rationalize. A reality that just is.

The final tour destination seemed to matter less and to matter more. I skipped through the next twenty or so songs in my library, nothing suitable to the mood. I landed on "I'm Old Fashioned" by John Coltrane, largely from resignation. I slumped in that rare numbness in which a single thought has disabled the machinery of thinking. Almost a welcome release, if not so sad. The left corner of my forehead pressed to the window, the black-gray road blurred past for nearly thirty minutes. On the horizon, two spires sketched an outline in the sky. My pulse quickened. My nerves frizzed. "You only get hurt when you have expectations," my mother once said. Of course, she had offered this insight when, at age thirteen, I had asked to attend a movie with a group of friends, two of them female. Disproportionate to the circumstances though her comments might have been, the axiom registered that day and stayed with me. I had expectations of the shrine, so, yes, I could be hurt. More disappointed than hurt, but the visceral expression of vulnerability draws no distinction.

The vehicle ambled into the parking lot, rocking side-to-side over uneven pavement. Before the hiss-snarl crank of the opening door, the driver explained we would have forty-five minutes, which sounded hurried, although one hour would have sounded too long. Passengers who had dozed off stretched in the aisle, blocking my path. Chatter among them about the best location for a photograph, about souvenirs for neighbors, chewed into my forty-five minutes. I imagined knocking them out of the way with comedic enthusiasm. I laughed both to myself and at myself, my impatience exposed as a cartoon.

Once outside, the elements produced a scene clipped from cinema: pewter clouds dappled with sunlight, a gentle rain, gusts sprinting in from every direction. Past others in fixed admiration of the architecture, past those slowed by the solemnity of the surroundings, I marched, my eyes on the entrance. One might have suspected the basilica soon would close, I walked with such purpose. I was, after all, on a mission.

I climbed the front stairs, each just steep enough to require more work from the hamstrings, possibly a design feature, a speed bump to pause a person before entering. I opened the doors. Almost every church welcomes you with the same scent of incense and wood polish. I selected a row on the left, close to the middle, and sat. I felt unreasonably tired, as if I had crawled the almost three million feet from the front door of my house to the pew. Tension had held me together for days. More like months and months. Now released from my body like carbon dioxide. Diaphragm expanded. Joints loosened. The setting began to disassemble me so completely, I worried I would crumple into a pile of Mr.-Potato-Head parts, the caretaker having to sweep me up at the end of the night.

I thought to myself: *I am here. Do the rest.*

7

MY HAND DID NOT CLINK.

After exiting the elevator on the floor of my office, you turn right and reach a glass door at the entrance of our suite. Each day, several times a day, I would grab the vertical, hollow, metal tube that serves as the handle, against which my wedding ring clinked perfectly. A tinny charge, like the light tap of a pick into ice, one of thousands of clattering, atmospheric notes you hear throughout your waking hours. A slight vibration through the bones of my hands, up my wrist, almost grazing my elbow. I never paid much attention to the sensation. Until it was gone.

I had removed my wedding ring on the day the divorce commenced. The first time back in the office, my left fingers wrapped thoughtlessly, soundlessly around the handle. A volt shot up my arm, into my chest, as if treated with a defibrillator powered by absence and silence. I put my right palm against the wall to steady myself for a few seconds. I looked behind me to see if anyone had noticed, not that anyone would.

A palpable, tactile, material change underway, in big and small ways. The ring, only part of the small.

Living alone, part of the big.

I immediately began my interregnum period, although interregnum refers to an interval, a middle segment bookended by a before and an after. Nothing seemed like the middle in those early weeks. Only an indefinite, unpredictable carousel ridden with one-day-at-a-time stoicism. I thought: *Is this my life now? Am I just leasing this phase on a month-to-month basis or should I buy more permanent real estate? If I know I am staying here for a while, should I get better furniture?*

Fortunately for me, I only had to worry about metaphorical furniture, not real furniture. I continued to stay in the house by myself, itself a weird, clumsy phenomenon, like living on the set of a canceled television program or in an abandoned amusement park. I returned each day, naturally expecting to hear a familiar greeting in a familiar voice. I adopted the bizarre habit of walking into every room on each floor. I would stand there for a few seconds, listening to the low drone of stasis and vacancy. I do not know what I thought would happen, that someone might jump out of the closet or from behind a dresser. Maybe I just had to confirm that I was, in fact, as alone as I felt.

The open space, not only physical. My home, a warehouse overstocked with personal freedom. I had grown so accustomed to my wife bouncing off of me— and I off of her—the minor, everyday questions that spin the turbine propelling life. ("Should I eat dinner before going to the gym or after?" "Should I finish reading tonight or just go to bed and finish tomorrow?") Without this dialogue, my time amounted to some odd, impossible combination of inertia and chaos. I was a pinball waiting to be launched in a machine without the bumpers and tubes and spirals. No impetus. No direction. A lot less fun. Perhaps one can be too unencumbered.

"Take advantage of it," some advised of this (outwardly) carefree, indeterminate period, as if bestowed a sabbatical from domesticity. For me, taking advantage meant eating Lucky Charms for dinner, since my metabolism had started to burn like a steamship furnace and I could not stomach real food. So, yes, a slight thrill as I jammed another bowl to the brim with marshmallow stars and diamonds and clovers, but also a seizing truth: No one cared if I ate dinner, much less what I ate. No one cared about much of what I did or did not do over the course of a day. Liberating, maybe. Empty and frightening, definitely.

Of course, family and friends cared about me, if not my choice of cereal. I became to them like a pet they took turns watching while the owner traveled. They made sure I drank enough water and went out for walks and napped in rooms set at the right temperature. They brought me along on errands. Like a pet, I communicated very little, more in noises and expressions than words. They let me flump in the corner while they continued with their business. Exactly what I required. Around activity, without having to participate.

So as not to deplete totally the reservoir of goodwill supplied by those closest to me, I started to reach out to a wider circle of friends to fill them in on the news. If nothing else, doing so occupied my time. Like a hobby, but instead of gluing together a model airplane or affixing stamps in a book, I recited the unexpected tale of my crumbling marriage. Quasi-Homeric, without the scale. Semi-bardic, without the lyre. Actually, neither. Much dryer and more straightforward, like a report filed with the Federal Emergency Management Agency. The storytelling medium did, though, create some helpful distance. I became a character in the action. The events happened to someone with my name. I could sit in the audience and say, "Too bad," and ask, "Can you believe it?" I could ascend from a seat in the orchestra, up to the mezzanine, then to the very back of the balcony, looking down on the stage from a fresher, wider vantage, the scenes more fluid, a little less intense. Faintly, my recounting mirrored a practice as old as—and at the foundation of—history, itself: trying to understand.

I did not understand. At least not then. Perhaps not ever. No one did.

I needed my friends for more reasons than I could estimate: encouragement, release, steadiness, kindness. Another reason? To hear their surprise. The "Whoa!" The "What?" The "Really?" Their shock affirmed my (temporary) sanity. Or that we all were crazy. Either way, we united in dumbfounded solidarity amidst what seemed like unreality.

"What's it like?" or some similar question, each person eventually asked.

I experimented liberally with selections from the Lexicon of Personal Calamity, trying out different adjectives along the way, partly to maintain my own interest.

Cyclonic. Phantasmagoric. Hallucinatory. Woebegone. Impenetrable.

Each word applicable, I suppose, by some fraction. All of them so inadequate, as well. I never did discover the right one, the one that would have me call off the search, the alpha-and-omega of descriptors securely in my hands. I eventually extended beyond single words to full sentences. I drafted simile after simile, attempting to come up with witty, trenchant lines. A game, really. A challenge to keep my own attention on a monotonous essay, as well as to remind everyone around me that I remained my same sardonic, deprecating self and, therefore, in no more danger of immolation than any previous point.

"What's it like?" they asked.

"I feel like a ghost haunting my own life."

"I feel like a walking Mayan prophecy."

"I feel like I accidentally stepped onto the stage during a production of *Who's Afraid of Virginia Woolf?*"

"Have you lost weight?" someone asked.

"I'm in the process of dropping a little over one-hundred pounds."

The person laughed and said, "Well, at least you still have your sense of humor."

"She won't get that in the divorce," I snapped back.

More laughter.

After the laughter, advice. Lots and lots of advice. All well-meaning and deeply appreciated, but some a touch misguided and tonally dissonant. Certain people could not help but project their dissatisfaction onto me.

"You've been given a gift."

"What I wouldn't do to be you."

The commentary revealed the passive, status-quo, near-contentment to which some had submitted themselves. Not motivated enough to initiate action, but if circumstance somehow coughed up opportunity, they would grab it and speed away. In the meantime, they lived vicariously through me, as heard in their quick-draw recommendations.

"You should move away as soon as possible. Get yourself into the city. That's what I would do."

"I can't move," I explained. "Everyone who loves and resents me lives here."

"When you get back out there," another suggested, "you need at least three."

To this day, I still have no idea what this individual meant by "three," but I was too apprehensive to ask for an explanation. I also did not want to know the answer.

"I really wouldn't wish this on anyone," I said.

"You say that now, but you'll see," someone replied, which sounded Delphic and ominous, even though he intended quite the opposite.

From those who already had seen, so to speak, those who had gone through their own divorces, I received more grounded counsel. Generous human beings opened up about their struggles, not unlike spotting a stranger on crutches after you have suffered the same injury. You ask about the precipitating incident, then reveal your own. ("Ruptured mine rescuing a crate of puppies from a house fire. That's a lie. I did it playing basketball.") You show your scar. You detail your recovery, when you finally returned to your old routines, your old self. In the same manner, those gracious divorce veterans had shown me their scars, had told me of how they had resumed their back-on-their-feet lives. They resided squarely on the "other side" and promised I one day would join them. The "other side," almost utopian, a sanctuary for gentle woodland creatures, free of predators. The destination seemed more realistic and appealing than the smoky, sweaty, strobe-lighted bacchanal yearned for by those still in marginally happy relationships.

An ungrateful human being, I took exception with this empathy. I essentially entered into a love-hate relationship with universality. Yes, on one hand, so comforting to hear how I did not represent the first or last person ever to encounter a separation. On the other hand, I disliked having my marriage minimized, normalized, categorized, as if manufactured on an assembly line and beset by the factory recall that removes one-out-of-two of the same model from the marketplace.

"Mine was different," I wanted to tell others. "You don't get it."

But it was not different. I was the one who did not get it. Difficult, at first, to acknowledge the ordinariness of your life.

For a while, I kept universality locked in this dysfunctional, no-win relationship. "Console me with examples of how much my divorce is like everyone else's," I might have demanded, like some bloated monarch with a jester or a drunken sea captain with his cabin boy. "Now let me tell you why you are so wrong." Fortunately, universality has no feelings to hurt. If possible, though, I imagine it would have tiptoed around me.

I also consulted several sources. Books. Articles. Question-and-answer sessions posted on the internet. Some of questionable credibility and expression. I read stories with titles like, "Surviving Divorce: The Dos and Don'ts" and "Life After Divorce: Survival Strategies." Only months earlier, if I had come across these pieces, I would have thought: *Thank God I don't have to worry about that.* Wrong. Enough materials out there for classification as a genre or an industry. Some of the entries, clarifying. Other entries? Like passages from a diary no eyes ever should see. Or worse, like those misanthropic manifestos dug up in the homes of disgruntled hermits on crime sprees. Bullet-pointed battle cries baying for vengeance, with the vengeance usually expressed as body-toning, higher-end style and flirtations with much younger men and women. Humorous, both intentionally and unintentionally. Overall, I found the information somewhat lacking.

So, I searched according to a different term: "Losing your spouse."

I could relate much more readily to those who wrote of departure without the chance of return. Those bleeding from the one-day-here-next-day-gone tear. Those who could not conceive of filling or bridging the chasm with another element, so they only described the bottomlessness. I felt guilty relying on these reflections. Their partners, lost to illness or age or an accident. I had not earned the right to share in their pain. I wondered: *Is mine even grief? Is this more like punishment? Is this punishment for the shortcomings cited by my soon-to-be-former wife, the shortcomings I wish I had been made aware of over the years, rather than only during those final days? Or had I been made aware all along, but did not pay enough attention to them? Or were mine just otherwise forgivable failings that suddenly—and perhaps conveniently—had been magnified, so that she could give herself permission to begin a new life?*

I felt confused. And angry. And sad.

These words, simpler than the flashier modifiers I had used in conversations with my friends. Simpler than my similes. Still not accurate enough, not true enough. I suppose if someone had asked, "What's it like?" and if I had not concerned myself with answering in a deadpan, enlightened style, I would have said with plaintive honesty, "I don't know." Because "it" encompassed many words, all at once. Because "it" changed from day-to-day. Even so, I would have stated with complete certainty, "Whatever it is, it is worst at night."

When my last phone call ended each evening—usually with my brother and usually around ten—I began the portion of the day I dreaded. Yes, many had told me, "Call at any hour, day or night, if you ever need to talk," but I could not inconvenience them. Every now and then, I would reach out to my friends on the West Coast, the three-hour time difference enough of a lag to qualify the discussion as commonplace.

All alone, I uninhibitedly splayed myself out on the couch in shorts and t-shirts I never would let the public see. My stomach, released from hours of contraction. My back curved in, posture sent home for the day. Such a mess. A human being of near-liquid constitution. I thought: *This is divorce*, sometimes with a question mark at the end of the sentence, sometimes with a declarative period. I probably felt more divorced at night, because during those hours, I had felt more married. The two of us, talking about our days, going through our upcoming schedules, maybe touching on plans in the not-so-distant future. Suddenly, none of that. Just silence.

In the absence, my mind returned not to our wedding day or vacations or holidays, even though photos from those events still sat on the bookshelves and end tables. No, I remembered the Saturday night, two weeks after we had moved into our first apartment, shopping in a generic discount store for shelves to hold our extra soap and razors in the bathroom. As we put the cheap contraption together, I thought to myself: *What will the next bathroom look like?* Because there would be a next bathroom. And several more bathrooms after that. And that prospect brought me happiness.

I remembered when we both caught the flu one March. We lumbered into the pharmacy to buy supplies, literally propping each other up in the aisles. Back home, we watched bad comedies, laugh-coughing, the jokes taken to heights they otherwise would not have scaled without the assistance of our fevers. Later, when we would see one of those movies on television, we would comment fondly, "Remember how sick we were?"

The marriage, thousands and thousands of these snippets, the tree-falling-in-the-woods catalogue of a life together. Since the only person who had witnessed and experienced them had disappeared, had they happened? Did they matter? Were those years worth anything, since they did not keep adding up to something? It all seemed a little lost.

In place of a relationship I had not expected to end, I now had nights that dawdled like the last party guest you wish would just head home. Astonishing how quickly two in the morning becomes three in the morning, as if the quiet clears the roadway for the minutes to complete the course in record time. Then, in the distance, not long before five, the first train would whistle the new day. I would breathe in defeat, another evening having gotten the better of me. My only hope, that sleeplessness eventually would gain so much weight, I would buckle under a pile of hours and hours.

One night, lying on my bed around one in the morning, rain dribbled through the gutters outside the window. I thought: *How little separates me from the world? How little keeps me from splashing onto the ground like one of those raindrops, soaked into the concrete?*

Stop.

I had to stop. My musings had become crazier and—more alarmingly—incredibly pretentious. A raindrop? Really? I could tolerate the loneliness and the sadness and the insomnia, but I could not abide likening myself to a raindrop. The silence would eat me alive from the inside out. Or it would drive me to stupid raindrop metaphors. I had to do something.

I started to buy songs.

My wife and my personal musical tastes might have suffered collateral damage during our time together. We rarely played anything in the house, except around the holidays. Neither of us had said, "I don't like this," or, "Turn that off," when the other had put on a favorite track. Perhaps I had sneered or sighed at certain of her selections, which I now regret. In fact, she had bought me tickets to concerts for bands I liked, as I had done for her. We might have reverted to artists we both enjoyed, out of respect, I guess. We had a compromise collection. But what did I like? I might have forgotten.

On that rainy night, I typed in my credit-card information and opened my own account. I began with the Progenitor of Soul, the musician who had etched his image, note-by-note, into the Mount Rushmore of songwriters: Smokey Robinson. I downloaded *My World—The Definitive Collection*. To keep him company, I bought a greatest-hits album by one of his closest friends—the man to whom he referred as "Dad"—Marvin Gaye.

I put in my earphones, which from that second would become an almost-permanent appendage. I pressed play on "Yester Love." The opening percussion sounded like tripping and falling into the music. The horns blared an annunciation. The guitar plucked its bopping chords. Smokey sauntered in with a honey-sweet hum, until having the stage handed over to his elegant, supple vocals and the backing of The Miracles. I closed my eyes and settled into the pillow.

From that point forward, my nighttime ramblings would have to compete for attention with "Misty Blue" by Dorothy Moore and Al Wilson's recording of "I Won't Last a Day Without You," composed by the incomparable Paul Williams. The silence, no match for "Since I Lost My Baby" by The Temptations and "Never Can Say Goodbye" by Isaac Hayes.

Thanks to all of them, I felt a little less alone.

8

WITH ALL DUE RESPECT to Steven Soderbergh, I did not have a good Fourth of July.

Heading into the first holiday since my marriage had splintered, I should have anticipated problems. Maybe Independence Day's inherent informality had tranquilized me. Eating outdoors. Hot dogs on a grill. Fireworks in a distant sky. What could go wrong? Without the domestic-culinary rituals attached to Thanksgiving or the religio-secular pageantry associated with Christmas, July Fourth adopts an *ad hoc* quality. The day becomes either what you make of it or what others make available to you. The easiest holiday from which to absent yourself, as well. Just answer, "I've got plans," and from the hook you are released.

A little more foresight and I, too, would have had "plans" on that Fourth of July. I should have judged better the circumstances and myself.

When I opened my eyes that morning, I conducted a system check, like a flight crew prepping for takeoff. Knees? Fine. Shoulders? Sore, but functional. Heart rate? Slightly above normal. Some days, my frame creaked and cracked the sounds of an older man. Other days, I felt younger, strangely enough. Regardless, I had to determine how well I could hold it together during the upcoming hours.

When I had heard individuals apply to themselves the term "holding it together," I would experience one of those nanosecond spasms in which irritation comes out in a cough or a twitched facial muscle. Histrionics, I believed. A luxury not afforded to less self-conscious generations, as if my immigrant grandparents had worried about "holding it together" while battling extreme poverty and ethnic discrimination. Until I had to resort to "holding it together." Each day seemed charged by some despotic celestial being with the task of tearing me in two, perhaps because he or she required half a human to fill out a trophy case. The first shot of daylight through the blinds and an invisible instrument cinched into my ribs, clawing me open. Fighting it off—"holding it together"—demanded an extraordinary amount of energy, an energy doled out only in finite amounts, with no instructions for replenishment. Sleep did nothing. I barely ate. I would sense the depletion, a shrinking mass where the stomach meets the chest. I could read the internal gauge as it neared zero, a flashing red light on the dashboard of an automobile.

Going out in public drew even more thirstily from my reserves. Prior to any social engagement, I would estimate if I had enough in the tank to proceed without incident. I would calculate not just time, but location, number of people, comfort level with those present, potential for a swift exit. I canceled appointments without much warning. I slipped quietly out of functions well before the conclusions.

In those first minutes on that Fourth of July, the red light flickered. Empty. I could have backed out of my plans—should have, really—but I was not quite ready to surrender to an extended stay in bed, followed by an extended stay on the couch, concluding with a return to bed. I dislodged myself from the mattress, showered and dressed, a simple series of actions that felt like an Everest ascent. In the car, I began the short journey to my brother's house for a barbecue with family and a few friends, stopping first to retrieve my parents.

Small towns never appear quite as large as they do on Independence Day. Vestigial municipal squares and greens temporarily revived for ceremonies scored with peppy Sousa tunes, while children pedal bicycles decorated in red, white and blue streamers. I rode through several of these scenes on the way to my parents' home. None reached me.

Stepping on the walkway to the front door, my pants tangled up. Less to hug, the waistband slid down to a wider segment of my lower torso, the cuffs snagging my sneakers. My t-shirt just floated around me. Most of my clothes started to match my childhood wardrobe, the drawers stuffed full of still-too-big-for-me hand-me-downs from my brothers.

"Are you all right?" asked my father as soon as I entered.

"Fine," I said. The word out the right side of my mouth like a quick burst of smoke. I would not have known how to respond to me, not certain if my reply wanted to be pursued or abandoned.

"You look tired. Are you tired?" my mother asked.

"I'm fine." The *ine* vibrated against the roof of my mouth in a low, guttural hum.

Her illness might have muddied the waters that separate incapacity from willful refusal. She could not let go, either because she was sick or because she was, well, my mother.

"I think you're tired. You just look tired. Is something wrong?"

"I said I'm fine."

Too easily had I rediscovered the snappy irascibility of a teenager. I committed completely to the character with an adolescent sulk in a chair in the living room. (*Is something wrong? Really? Seriously? Is something right? That's the question.*) The screws of obligation turned more tightly into my temples, my jawbones bulging out as I bit down. My brand of self-centeredness usually collapses all of history into the singular instant in which only I live. Every unmet desire ever nurtured by humanity had fused into one: I had to exit that house and be alone. If this solitary need went unfulfilled a second longer, I would splatter across the furniture, splashes of me later having to be cleaned off framed family photos and lampshades. My obituary would read, "Man Explodes in Front of Parents on Holiday."

I laughed to myself. Ridiculousness usually marked the final stop before reason on the looping route of my consciousness. I breathed more slowly. Perspective regained. The worst had passed. I sat for a few more minutes. Rubbing my hands across my eyes, down my face, I tried to speak gently.

"You're right. I am tired. I just don't think I have it in me to go today. If you don't mind, I'll drop you off and head on my way."

Then, my mother said something.

I cannot recall her exact words. I probably had forced myself to forget in a preemptive act of self-defense, because if I had replayed precisely her otherwise innocuous statement, my reaction would appear objectively monstrous and galactically out of line. To paraphrase, she suggested—in a few, incisive sentences—that, due to recent events, I harbored anger toward women and that I had taken this anger out on her.

To say I lost control would stray from the truth, for I maintained a degree of control. I knew how I should have responded. I should have shrugged and ignored the comment, possibly adding, "You're right," but in a semi-benevolent tone that conveys, "You're wrong, but I see no way of convincing you of such, so I will detour onto a higher road." But I chose to respond differently, the "chose" highlighted in red. I opted for a confrontation.

Why?

Perhaps because my mother had managed to make the matter about her. Maybe because she had assigned to me failure with half of the species, as opposed to only one member. In doing so, she rather dismissively canopied my relationship under irresolvable female-male dynamics, although, to be fair, I would have gone crazier had she personalized her criticism. More than likely, as selfish as it may sound, after weeks of "holding it together," of walking the balance beam of equanimity, I just needed to get mad. My mother finally had given me the opportunity to do so.

"That is about the most insensitive thing anyone could have said to me right now."

A saner, sanitized paraphrase of my comment, I imagine, as I also did not record my contributions to the exchange. Loud and sharp, doused in kerosene and outrage, further sentiments poured from me, all the while thinking to myself: *I should not be doing this.* My mother did not retreat, formidable as ever. Arguments with her were not won or lost, just tabled without conclusion due to frustration. We had conducted one continuous, lifelong quarrel, with hiatuses of a year or more, until inevitably roused and resumed. On that July afternoon, the two of us had squared off in perhaps the final round of mother-son conflict. A small part of me appreciated her antagonism. Still herself, despite the disease. Still enough of herself for me to recognize we would achieve no closure. So, I just left, possibly doing so in semi-dramatic fashion. I cannot remember. Or I chose not to remember.

A few miles away from the house, I grabbed the steering wheel so manically it could have broken if comprised of lesser materials. *I was right*, I thought. *I was right*, unblinking, straight ahead. A few miles farther away, being right faded. My temperature dipped, the perspiration on my forearms and around my neck greasy and cold. What did it matter if I were right? I had squabbled with an ill woman, one who could not retaliate as well as she once could. Such a coward. Worse than having behaved so abominably, I had granted myself permission to do so. I had convinced myself: *I get to do this. I get to be a jerk.* My personal situation somehow had entitled me to act out, I had led myself to believe. So disgraceful.

No doubt, at my brother's home that afternoon, the conversation had turned to what transpired. The muttering beneath the grill crackle. The hushed comments between the toss of paper plates in the garbage can.

"Not cool of him to do that."

"Give the guy a break. He's been through a lot."

"It was bound to happen sooner or later."

Regrettably, I had welded myself permanently onto the day. Screwing up on a holiday virtually guarantees the tale of your weakness will resurface annually, like a retched ornament or a disliked relative.

"Remember the Fourth of July when he lost it on Mom?"

Back in my town, the streets and sidewalks steaming and swept of life, most people having scattered to their barbecues and swimming pools and not-frowned-upon day-drinking. I enjoyed the simple pleasure of access to almost every parking spot, of not having to put a quarter in the meter. As I walked to buy myself something to eat, I passed a couple, both a few years older than I, each in crisp shorts and untucked polo shirts. We did not know one another, but we recognized each other well enough from our daily patterns to nod as stranger-neighbors do. This interplay, however superficial, bothered me.

I placed my order at the deli and as I waited for my sandwich, I reviewed the nod as a slow-motion instant replay. The wife's eyebrows might have scrunched together judgmentally. The husband might have avoided direct eye contact. Had they heard of the divorce? Bad news, after all, zooms, while good news simply saunters. If so, did they assess blame, as many instinctively do without the benefit of a single fact? Maybe.

Over to my car, the dangling plastic bag whisking against my leg, I climbed in and shut the door. The thud hovered in the air for a few seconds, until lifting into a shrill, crackling note that just lingered in perpetuity. Having passengers would have absorbed the sound. Not then. Just a hollow, heated cabin. The echo raised another possibility behind that couple's disconcerting nod. I might have transformed into That Guy, the one seen by himself every day, whom others really do not know or care to know, but whose backstory becomes more curious on holidays. Those who spot him on a Thanksgiving morning or on an Easter afternoon wonder: *Does he have somewhere to go? Family? Friends?* Perhaps they concoct a scenario in which a colleague from his place of employment pities That Guy enough to invite him over, preparing the children in advance: "Larry from the office will be here, so be nice to him. He didn't have anywhere else to be."

When going about my daily business, would I now have to slip into the small talk between the card swipe and the goods exchange how I have a sizeable family, roots in the community and multiple cherished traditions, if only to sway eavesdroppers to discard their amateur serial-killer profiles? Should I have approached the nodding couple with whom I never before had spoken and said, "Before you judge me, let me tell you what happened"?

Judged or not judged, That Guy or not That Guy, if nothing else, I had become paranoid. Unnecessarily so, I eventually would see, since people have their own lives to lead, with little time for either the good or bad experienced by others. Even so, I still chose to shop in grocery stores several towns away, late in the evening, along with the other bachelors and divorced guys. This temporary paranoia did not even let me sit in the deli that afternoon to enjoy my sandwich, but rather brought me immediately back to my house. I usually ate standing up in the kitchen or in front of the television. On the celebration of the nation's birth, I decided to eat in the dining room, a space that otherwise acted as a repository for mail. No distractions of music or movies.

Just chewing in quiet. I thought: *Mastication is a funny word, no?* On the previous July Fourth, I might have verbalized such an observation to my wife.

No longer any point in delaying the inevitable, I draped my body over the couch. So strange. Everything bright and light outside—perfect, really—yet there I lay with the blinds closed, trying to talk myself into the uninterrupted viewing of the TCM lineup: *The Music Man* to *1776* to *Yankee Doodle Dandy*. Not a wholly unappealing way to burn through my afternoon, but I became fidgety. Just before five, I walked a few blocks to the local movie theater. Having not bothered to check the start times, my eyes scanned the options left-to-right, up-and-down. If more aware, I would have caught the teenager in the ticket booth, shoulders sagged, hands on the counter, with a snide, twisted half-grin that said: *You've only got one choice right now, buddy.* He was correct. I then spoke the saddest, loneliest words ever uttered by a man on Independence Day.

"One for *Magic Mike*, please."

On the Fourth of July, who attends a late-afternoon screening of a film about male strippers in Tampa? Two groupings of three women, giddily liberated from their normal suburban routines. And me. I sat in the last row, in the farthest seat, against the wall, embodying fully my role as creepy interloper. I cannot remember much about what I watched—again, with all due respect to Steven Soderbergh—only that it succeeded in meeting the criterion of "activity in a venue beyond my home."

The movie over, I fled the theater as if someone had yanked the fire alarm. Night had started to blanket the town, bringing with it the hope the day soon would end. I could put behind me my first holiday as a newly single person. Such an unfortunate set of hours. I had fooled myself into thinking I could coast through this transition without ever suffering or inflicting damage. Damage done is damage to be undone, I might have heard someone aphoristically spout. Or I might have made it up. Either way, the next morning, I would drive to my mother to apologize.

Closer to my house, I saw my father's car parked in front.

"What are you doing you here?" I asked, as if I did not know.

"Mom is worried about you. She wanted me to come check on you. She feels terrible."

"I feel worse. I shouldn't have done that. Come on in."

"I can go. I just had to make sure you were all right."

"Please come in."

My father had visited my home many times, but he paused at the entrance. He might have feared what he would see. Maybe a tower of dirty dishes in the kitchen sink. Or evidence of a budding Howard-Hughes lifestyle, tissue boxes in my closet and dusty mason jars on windowsills. Everything, though, appeared the same, perhaps too much so. My wedding photo still on the mantle. The furniture familiarly arranged. My wife's raincoat even hanging on the coatrack. The stage set for a husband very much in denial. My father and I sat across from one another. We each exhaled as if we had completed manual labor, like cleaning out an attic or tarring a roof. He had not come with a script. The miles he had traveled just to stop by, that was his message. We rested in the silence for a few minutes, the breath of another human being already somewhat alien within those walls.

"Needless to say, today wasn't one of my best, Dad. I should know better. It's not her."

"I'm not here for you to say you're sorry. You're our highest priority right now. Nothing else. She'll be fine."

"She just … She just struck a nerve."

"I know. In her own way, she knows, too. She is sorry."

"I just—"

No word could form. Some kind of kill switch triggered in my mouth. All of my blood and strength rushed toward "holding it together." My father could not look at me. Not out of shame. I just think he could not carry the image with him. Hard enough on him to see me shaken and sallow, sad and blank during the day. But the scene of me alone in the house, on the couch each night, gulping and lost, that would have haunted him.

Fireworks whistled and popped around us, the *deus-ex-machina* change-in-subject we both needed.

"Those sound like they are coming from right next door," he said.

"Not too far away. The field is just down the street."

"Do they hold the fireworks here like they do back in our town?"

"Mostly the same. I always remember the Fourth when I was about nine years old. You drove us to the football field. You stopped the car to let us out at the entrance and it dawned on me that you weren't coming with us. You thought I was old enough by then that I would rather be with my brothers. But I still wanted to go with you. I got upset."

"I remember that night."

"Without saying a word, you changed your plans. You parked the car and brought me in. We found a seat in the stands, right by our next-door neighbors."

"That's right. They would always go. They wouldn't miss it."

"I think I polished off their entire box of Cracker Jack."

"They didn't mind. They were always so nice."

"So were you, Dad. And here we are again on the Fourth of July."

Sitting in my living room, the two of us just listened to the fireworks. The high-frequency whirs. The cannon-ball booms. I could imagine the green and red tendrils of their short-burst lives, the gray plumes of their deaths. Not long after the cacophonous, rat-tat-tat finale, I followed my father from my front porch to his car, the smoke dissipating high above us in the navy night sky. Along the sidewalk, a parent passed us on his exit from the field, a balloon tied to his wrist, a sleepy three-year-old slung over his shoulder.

"I feel like that kid," I said. "At least you didn't have to carry me back today."

My father laughed. Before he drove off, I asked him to call me when he made it home, which he did.

"Someone would like to talk to you," he said, handing the phone to my mother.

"Are you mad at me?" she asked.

"No, Mom. You should be mad at me."

"I'm not. I'm sorry if I upset you."

"I'm the one who is sorry. I shouldn't have acted that way. I'm just not myself these days. It's no excuse. I get upset and I don't understand why."

"I know. I don't understand why I act certain ways either."

I bit down hard, swallowed hard. "Goodnight, Mom."

"I love you," she said.

I went to bed less anxious, more at peace than previous evenings, likely due to having finally lost my temper, to having discharged so much repressed emotion. Uncertainty usually suffocated me unconscious each night. (Well, uncertainty and Tylenol PM.) Finances. Relationships. The location of the county-run nursing home in which I would die alone, with no next of kin to notify. All so uncertain. When drowsiness finally cascaded into my hands, down through my legs, my last wish of each day: something certain. One solid element that just might start a new foundation. As the Fourth of July gave way to the less-notable Fifth of July, I believed I had found atoms of certainty.

I never again would behave as I did that afternoon.

I would try to do more for my mother.

9

THE TWO OF US WILL DIE. Many years in the future, more than likely. One before the other. One of us will learn of the other's passing. Maybe the survivor will read about the event in a newspaper or however obituaries will be published in the coming decades. Perhaps a mutual friend will call or email or text or whatever, "I thought you would like to know." The one of us left behind will have a reaction or a reflection in that instant. What exactly? Surprise? Surprise with how deeply or how shallowly the news hits, a shrug over a loss already mourned years ago or astonishment with the inadequacy of that prior grieving? Will the one of us still around think back to our beginning and our middle? Or just the end? Will the one of us still around go about that day only mildly disturbed, as if a famous musician or an actor had expired? Will the one of us left behind feel the need to pay respects or visit the grave? Or will the one of us left behind feel nothing, the hunks of earth already piled and packed on the relationship years earlier in a courtroom?

These were among the first thoughts through my mind in the initial days and weeks after the divorce ball had started to roll. Strange, really. And dark. Maybe as my head had inventoried the prospective shared experiences that never would come to be, I naturally began at the terminus and worked my way backward. I always had assumed we would be with one another at the end, either meeting my own conclusion or bearing witness to hers. No longer.

We did not talk. We barely communicated electronically. Even then, only to let her know about the delivery of an important piece of mail or for her to let me know she had to retrieve some items from the house. Our exchanges, cordial and exceedingly polite. If an outsider had reviewed the content, we each would receive commendations for outstanding customer service.

She did once write, "I never wanted it to end like this," which threw me, since—in my mind—the marriage was not meant to end. I thought we had given one another a nearly inexhaustible supply of time. Time to grow. Time to work on our issues. Time to pull ourselves out of ruts. Time to realize the benefits of sacrifices made along the way. Perhaps my greatest misperception, believing the marriage was more durable than it ultimately proved to be.

I did think about her. Rather frequently, if honest. How could I not after being together for so long? I worried about her, which perhaps adopted an overly paternalistic tone, as if she required my support to survive. Not true. If anything, I always had viewed ours as an egalitarian apportionment of care and concern. She watched out for me. I watched out for her. I might have been wrong about this "egalitarian apportionment," because I have come to understand I was wrong about quite a bit. That I did not detect a problem is, in itself, a problem. Maybe I had assumed our relationship worked so well, because it worked for me. Maybe I did not examine closely enough how well it worked—if at all—for her.

If truthful, when I thought of her, I might have thought more about us as a couple. And in thinking of us, was I really thinking only of myself? Of how I dealt with the absence? Of how I could have corrected the mistakes I might not even have known I had made? Perhaps. Show me the divorce in which the word selfish does not get inserted at least once and I will introduce you to a giant serpent from a lake in Scotland. Yes, admittedly, selfishness might have dripped into my consideration of her. An error worth filing away for exploration when not crushed under the weight of one's own overpowering ego.

Hard to unwind two lives intertwined so thoroughly for so long. Or maybe not.

One day, the completed Case Information Statement arrived at my house. Paperwork generally breeds resentment. Divorce-related paperwork breeds a virulent resentment. An emotionally painful procedure adds strands of tedium and offense with every page and form. The Case Information Statement calls for each party to estimate independently the assets and expenses of married life. Utility bills. Groceries. Everything in as much detail as possible. The two then undergo reconciliation. Ours matched up almost to the cent. When I reviewed the document, with the numbers all in a line, my heart shrank a little. I always had hated math in school. My worst subject. Never did I hate math as much as on that Case Information Statement. Simple arithmetic applied to a union that supposedly defied calculation. The indivisible had become too easily divisible.

Again, I worried about her. My care, genuine, I believed, even as the sentiment started to approximate phantom-limb syndrome. One can fool oneself only so much. When the murk of selfishness and conceit and fear would lift, when I would find myself alone, without an audience or advocates, I still cared about her, irrespective of her care for me. If I had meant as much at the beginning, I would have to try to mean as much at the end. I would have to try to mean as much even as all of it—the divorce, the Case Information Statement—felt wrong. But there is not much to do about certain wrongs, other than accept them.

Over time, I stopped concerning myself if my former wife and I would run into one another or about what I would say or how my post-us life compared to hers. An unconscious method of self-preservation on my part. Or maybe just that way it is. Like it or not, my incidental relationships, such as with the person who swiped my identification at the gym, had started to develop more consistency and depth than the one with the woman once my partner. Over time, she became more abstract in my mind. I would describe her almost as a high-school student might a character from a book in English class. Sorry to say, because she had been one of the last figures whom I wished to have relegated to abstraction and memory.

10

LIFE TAKES AND LIFE GIVES, about as unimaginative an observation as one can make. True, nevertheless. When the taking and the giving occur in a single transaction, the red ink in the ledger initially takes over the whole page, so you see little else. Eventually, eyes adjust. The crimson lightens and, as it does, a sense of balance comes into focus, with it the understanding: *Well, I lost "X," but I gained "Y."*

The divorce took from me in terms of day-to-day synergy and longer-term plans. In return, I received time. Lots and lots of unstructured, uncommitted time. What to do with it?

People provided suggestions. All helpful, either because of the practicality—"You could volunteer somewhere or maybe learn a new language"—or the laugh-inducing impracticality—"Change your name and open a bed-and-breakfast in Majorca." Amusing insights into the do-over fantasies of those around me. Many seemed to have sunk a surprising amount of thought into their escape plans, as if they were career criminals ready to flee as soon as the authorities caught up to them. Fantasy living can become a heedless appetite at an all-you-can-eat buffet. I did not have the stomach for fantasy.

Not too much deliberation required regarding how I would spend my excess time. The conclusion of my marriage coincided with my mother's faltering health. My mother, for one, certainly would have interpreted the intersection of events as authored from above. My personal entanglements had untangled, while the duties related to her care multiplied. After my outburst on July Fourth, I made the conscious decision to do more for her. What that meant, I had no idea.

None of us did. The sickness drops you in rough, open waters with no sense as to your proximity to land. My family would ask among ourselves: "Are we closer to the beginning or to the end?" "Will this have to get worse before it gets better?" We would try to educate ourselves, reading articles, speaking with others whose loved ones had faced Alzheimer's disease and dementia. We would speculate as to her status based on behavioral patterns—"She doesn't even try to remember anyone's name anymore"—then float some makeshift solution—"Maybe we come up with a schedule for when each of us visits, so she has more consistent activity." We likely lagged several steps behind in the care guidelines, but not out of negligence. I think we hoped to preserve normalcy for as long as possible. We wanted one more birthday or one more holiday that resembled those that had come before them. Once gone, lost forever.

When we aimed to do more for her, we also aimed to do more for my father, the one shouldering a planet of responsibilities. We worried less about what we observed in my mother and more about that which we did not see, that which my father concealed from us, so that our days might breathe a little more freely.

"How is Mom today?" we would ask.

"Fine," he would say. "Everything is fine."

"Fine," the most disquieting of adjectives, one of blaring omission. Even a few details, however depressing—"She screamed at the mailman again," or, "She only wears the same sweater"—would have reassured us more than "fine." Only the most heartbreaking of incidents and exchanges churned beneath that broad generalization. In fairness, the situation likely had grown too enormous, too painful for him to analyze, as if he gripped hot sand and we had asked him to describe each grain as it fell through his fingers. Cruel to live with the decay of that which you love the most in the world. For my father, part of the deal. The beginning. The middle. The end. All what he had promised. The closest the man ever came to a complaint? "I almost have forgotten what she was like before all of this. Such an awful disease."

My brothers, accompanied by their families, regularly and frequently swarmed my parents' house. Their children supplied my mother with her greatest happiness. They would run around and play games and tell stories about school and sports and concerts.

My mother loved the company, the kinetic glee. Until she did not. The running around and playing games suddenly would unnerve her for no reason other than having smashed into the rigid barriers of her illness. An uncontrollable force—however positive—had intruded upon her secure environment, tripping a wire no one could see. My brothers carefully would take their children aside and explain, "It's not you. She's just not feeling well." Too bad she could not have enjoyed her grandchildren more. Too bad they would not know the grandmother who would have brought them to plays. Or who would have transformed a simple after-school pick-up into a spontaneous odyssey. Or who would have unspooled their family's otherwise ordinary history into a collection of folk tales.

Good friends dart toward your misfortune, not away. Again, unimaginative, but true. A number of my mother's longtime friends rushed in her direction, having monitored her slide as closely as they would their own family members. They organized meals with other acquaintances, surrounding her with light-hearted conversations in agreeable settings. They paid visits to the house. They encouraged her to join them on outings, as she had done for them in the past and certainly would have done had circumstances reversed themselves. When edged just beyond the locus of her comfort, though, my mother snapped. Her friends took her combativeness without protest. Her reaction stung them, no doubt, but they never wavered. They returned to her, unshaken and undeterred. Impossible to measure my gratitude for them, only to say that on the scales of life, their kindness outweighed the challenges.

Amidst the friends and grandchildren and brothers and sisters-in-law and supremely devoted father, what did I have to offer?

I initially functioned as a type of utility player, available to plug a hole in the lineup. If my father had a late meeting on a Wednesday night, I would stay at the house until he returned. If my mother needed new clothes, I would take her shopping. I tried to pop in as often as my schedule permitted. On those impromptu calls, I sometimes would find her sitting in her rocking chair, just looking out the window. Or thumbing through the same magazine she had been reading for weeks. Or losing herself in her high-school yearbook, the faces from her past more consoling than those in her present. She also would organize old photos, with different piles spread out on the dining-room table.

"Look at this," she said, as she showed me a picture of her mother. "Did you know this lady?"

Failure. Not despite, but because of her exuberance during these brief stops, I felt as if I had failed her. ("It's so good to see you. I was just thinking about you. What can we do?") Such modest gestures on my part—really, the very least I could do—filling a few minutes here and there. Yet the gestures disproportionately delighted her, which broke my heart in a new way.

I had to do more. Again, what?

Rather than consult experts or scan articles to find the activity suited for one at her stage of the ailment, I decided to follow the example set by the person who always seemed to know how to respond to another in distress: my mother.

For example, when I had wallowed in some dopey high-school malaise, she would say, "I've got an idea. Let's go somewhere." She would get me out of the house, maybe to a luncheonette or an ice cream shop. The location, not extravagant, but always animated by a story.

"This reminds me of a place we would go when I was around your age," she would tell me. "The big department stores back then had restaurants, all so stylish. Men in business suits and women in dresses. There were sparkling counters and chrome stools, just like here, with the customers crowded in on lunch breaks or shopping excursions. Very civilized, though. I felt as if I were on vacation and at a stage play at the same time, listening to the buzz, wondering what each did for a living. I told myself, 'When I'm older, I'll have a job where I can have lunch here whenever I want.'"

Maybe I would start to open up about whatever had troubled me at that time. Maybe not. And if not, my mother would continue.

"If you could go anywhere in the world right now, where would it be?" she might have asked.

"I don't know," I probably answered in my gravelly, teenage mumble.

"No? I ask myself all the time, ever since I was your age. I would think of a location—say, London—then imagine how I would get there from wherever I was right then. Let's say I was sitting in a lecture at college. I would walk myself through the journey, step-by-step. Catching the bus to the airport. Waiting at the terminal. Boarding the plane. Getting to my hotel. Finally, standing by the Thames or outside Westminster Abbey. A few times, I did it, too. Not London, but I would wake up and think, *I'd like to see the ocean today.* I would cancel my plans and drive down to the beach. I would spend just a few hours there and then head back. Happy I did it. Happy to be home."

I likely did not react, my attention dug into my lunch or dessert.

"Do you think your mother is crazy?" she might have asked.

"Not based on this," I would have said, but with enough wryness to defuse the disrespect.

"Ha," she would have laughed. "Well, what is the point of being able to go somewhere whenever you want unless you actually do it?"

My mother's efforts had succeeded back then, as I had forgotten for a little while what had bothered me in the first place. I also still could recall what she had shared. Now, at nearly eighty years old, she squared off with a real predicament, not one ignited by misfiring adolescent synapses. The methods perhaps not up to such an enormous test, I nevertheless dusted off the manual my mother, herself, had written.

Wait … Did you hear it? The announcement over the loudspeaker in the background?

"Paging Doctor Freud. Doctor Freud, please head immediately to the story."

Allow me to address the Oedipal Elephant in the Room. Yes, I understand the analysis one could conduct rather neatly: wife exits, so husband replaces her with his mother. The roaming tragic chorus could add, "I bet his wife was just like his mother," or, "Maybe his wife never could live up to his mother." No, nothing quite so D.H. Lawrence-*esque* at work. At least, I hope not.

Regardless, at my parents' house one afternoon during an unannounced visit, I said to my mother, "I thought we might go somewhere today. What do you think?"

"Sounds good to me."

She fretted for a few minutes about what she should carry with her. Purse. Cash. Keys. We checked and re-checked every locked door and window. Finally in my car, we began our drive. London, out of the question. The ocean also too far.

"Do you know where we are going?" she asked.

"I think you'll like it."

"If you say so, I trust you."

A few towns away, we stopped at a restaurant with the features of establishments from her youth: a counter with red stools swiveling on iron posts, decorative wainscoted ceiling, white tiles across the walls, polished, dark-wood booths. The retro ensemble splashed like a pebble in the still pond of my mother's memory, ring after ring of concentric circles rippling out until reaching her face in a smile. From timid imposter to her assertive and friendly self, she became, if just for a minute.

"So good to see you," she said to the hostess, a college-aged young woman who probably spent her shifts withstanding grievances about wait times and seating options.

"Aren't you nice?" she said. "I wish everyone greeted me like that."

"They don't? Well, they should. I'm with him today." She pointed to me.

"I think I've got the perfect table for the two of you."

She led us to our seats. As I reviewed the menu, my mother's head bobbed like that of a baby bird, taking in everything around her. She said, "I've never been to a place like this."

In the not-too-distant past, I would have corrected her. I might have replied, "Sure you have. You've been here many times." During those early stages of the disease, I had believed accuracy still mattered, that words or descriptions were no different than misplaced items, which, once back in her possession, she would hold on to even more watchfully. So wrong and shortsighted of me. Anger and irritation mixed in as well, if honest. Now when alone, just one-on-one, my mother and I had to re-learn how to communicate with one another. More to the point, I had to develop greater patience. Patience with the imprecision and the imperfection and the irrelevance and the repetition. Lots and lots of repetition. In truth, far less patience demanded of me during this period of her life than she showed me during my infancy, my adolescence … well, just about every period of my life.

When she said, "I've never been to a place like this," I resisted my inclinations and instead replied, "You haven't? It just seemed like somewhere you would enjoy."

"You know what this reminds me of?" she said.

"No. What?"

"A place I've been before, years ago, I think. In one of those big buildings downtown."

We were off. Encouraged rather than admonished, my mother would guide listeners on digressive tours through earlier chapters. Certain stories made more sense than others, both in their construction and their pertinence. The trail, though zigzagging, pointed toward a definite destination: connection. My mother wanted to forge a connection with the other person, as she had done so well in her better days. As her faculties slowed down, wore down, she called on the only material in which she had confidence: the more distant past. She would return there, to growing up with her brother and sisters, to her parents, to organizing her theater group, to teaching high school and writing for newspapers. She hoped that somewhere back there, the other person might discover something useful.

The two of us finished our meals that late afternoon. My mother left more on her plate than I would have preferred, given her sporadic eating habits and

diminishing weight. ("I'm just not that hungry today.")
She bid an enthusiastic farewell to her new friend, the
hostess. On the drive home, she said, "That was nice."

"I'm glad you liked it. We'll have to do it again."

And we did. I attempted to plan a somewhat consistent schedule of modest adventures. The sites had
to strike a balance between the familiar and the new.
Enough to comfort her. Enough to interest her. What
might have worked one day would not the next for no
identifiable reason, for no reason she could articulate.
We would experiment with some attractions, like with
a trip to a local arboretum. On that afternoon, only
a few yards down the flagstone footpath to the rose
bushes, I sensed her rejection. Her knuckles folded and
retracted into fists. Her posture stiffened.

"Do you like this place?" she asked in that disap-
proving tone I remembered so well from my youth. "Say
the word and I'm ready to go home whenever you are."

I crossed the arboretum off the list. As the weeks
and months passed, more and more places crossed
off the list. Like floodwaters, the illness swallowed up
the geography where my mother felt safe, narrowing
the acceptable locales to only a few. As the weeks and
months passed, darkness also invaded. The sun would
set and her mood would dim. Like a lunar tide, her
anxiety would rise with the appearance of the moon.
Panicked. Feverish with nuclear irrationality. Getting
her out of the house at that time, a fool's errand. But I
played the fool. I tried to convince her—probably too

aggressively—to have dinner, to go to one of our usual spots, guaranteeing her nothing would go wrong.

"How could you do this to me?" she yelled through tears. "I trusted you."

My mother felt betrayed. I felt diabolically thoughtless. All "road to hell" and "good intentions" and such, as the saying goes. "Play the hand you're dealt," as another saying goes. The hand dealt to us had decreased to daylight activities, to only a few territories within the shortest of drives. We played it.

On weekend afternoons, I picked her up. My father stayed at the house, not because we had not included him, nor because he had something else to do. My mother insisted a person wait behind to protect her home from theft. In nicer weather, we drove to the park only two miles away, the one in which she had walked with her parents and siblings as a little girl.

"This is a good choice," she said.

We usually took a lap around the lake, then down to the playground and back. She said hello to passersby as if she knew them. ("So good to see you again!") Some reciprocated the warmth. When ignored, my mother looked at me, twisted up the left corner of her mouth and shrugged with her palms turned upward, as if to say: *What are you going to do?* She paused to pet one or two of the dogs pawing at her ankles. ("Aren't you a good little guy?") After the park, the two of us went to the coffee shop.

"I think I like this place, right?" she said, as we pulled into the parking lot.

"You do."

The staff could not have treated her more kindly. They sometimes prepared her favorite drink—green tea latte—before we even reached the register. My mother chatted with the barista. ("You're so good at that.") We sat and talked for a few minutes. She enjoyed watching the other customers waiting in line, the high-school students gathered at tables to finish their weekend assignments.

"They're like us," she said as she motioned to an older couple relaxing in nearby armchairs.

"Not exactly. I think they're husband and wife." I had to revert to my sterner, instructive self and set the record straight on this point. "I'm your son."

"That's right," she said, staring at me for a few seconds, sunlight refracted in her sky-blue irises, the effect a whirling vortex. Behind them, a gasping recollection. This, the moment she ordinarily would have relayed knowledge or an experience or history. But she could not. She could not put those thoughts together. The moment, just silence between us.

"Should we head back?" I asked.

Our beverages in hand, we had one last leg on the itinerary: the pharmacy a few doors down in the same complex as the coffee shop. We perused the seasonal displays, usually just two aisles, the shelves stocked with Christmas wrapping or Easter baskets or, in the summer, sunscreen and plastic beach toys. Every now and then, she fell in love with one of the themed stuffed animals, like a Snoopy posing as Santa Claus or hugging Woodstock as they exchanged Valentines.

"I like him. Should we get him? I would give him to you," she said.

"I like him, too, but maybe next time."

"Well, we can't leave without those other things, right?"

My mother forgot so much, but she always remembered our reason for having entered the pharmacy. We would buy two bags of Lifesavers. One day, I tried to get away with purchasing only a single bag. She caught me.

"We get two, don't we? We always get two."

We then returned to the house, my father waiting for us as if we had completed a much lengthier, far more arduous journey. In the kitchen, she ritualistically emptied the Lifesavers into the clear, glass bowl in the center of the table. The three of us sat on the stools and finished our drinks, having brought one back for my father.

"What did you two do today?" he asked.

"We had a good time," my mother said.

We did, as best we could. But as I stared into my cup, moving it in a circle, the last of the liquid swirling hypnotically, faint desolation crept into my jaw, into my chest. Probably some awareness that we would not have many more minutes, the three of us together, around that table. That is life, though. Something else. Maybe because whatever I had tried to do for her, none of it would be enough. And to pretend as if whatever I had tried to do for her even approached being enough struck me as the worst lie I ever could tell.

11

"DO YOU LIVE WITH ANYONE?"

"No, not anymore."

"You should live here."

"No, thank you. I'm happy in my house."

"But you said you're alone. You should just stay here."

"Maybe one day. Just not today."

12

SO SINGLE-MINDEDLY had I entered Sainte-Anne-de-Beaupre, I neglected to take in the architecture, the aesthetics. With a break in my thoughts, I scanned around me, above me.

More than a church. More like a living organism. Not designed and constructed, but conceived and gestated, the interior decorated with the intricacies of a pale blood vessel or the cavity of a bone. Strapping marble pillars sprouted from the ground like trees, the branches merging with one another in elaborate arches. The ceiling curved into a canvas for a mosaic of amber and copper and ivory squares. On the edges of this geometry, human figures frozen in the stop-motion depiction of ecclesiastical trials and tributes.

Believer or non-believer, a person would have to feel somewhat moved, unless rotting inside.

And yet, at that minute, I felt entirely unmoved.

My heartbeat, slow and steady. My mind just as easily could have alternated between tasks on a daily to-do list and the larger issues I had traveled to address: pick up dry cleaning, pay the water bill, reconcile my divorce in the context of my outstanding time on earth, look into switching cable providers, etc. You never feel quite as soulless as when emotionally inert in a place intended to stir the blood and stoke the spirit. If I could feel nothing there, in that instant, then where and when? Ever? A bit worrying.

I never have taken a drama class, but I have heard of a rudimentary exercise in which a would-be actor concentrates on his or her saddest moment in order to mimic honest sentiment for the audience. Manipulative and gratuitous, perhaps, but not irrelevant in my case. I cast my mind back to my saddest moment, if only to affirm I was, in fact, alive. Not a single second wasted searching my archives. I had recognized my saddest moment as it had occurred.

Not the day of the official divorce, although I would not rank that occasion among my favorites. I could not say I rose early, because I never fell asleep. Around two in the morning, I had given up on rest. The day did not wake me, but rather I woke it, which began our relationship on fairly weird terms. We would not recover. The day and I would not feel right with one another from that point forward.

Before putting my feet on the floor, I hit play on "I Am the Sea," the opening track of The Who's *Quadrophenia*, probably my all-time favorite album. I listened start-to-finish as I pulled myself together. The band had never let me down. They would have to get me through a few tough hours.

I drove to the proceeding by myself, even though multiple family members had offered to accompany me. I showed up as early as possible. I did not wish to risk bumping into my wife in the parking garage, the two of us then having to walk in together, forcing ourselves into awkward small talk. Not too many good reasons to visit a courthouse, unless you view jury duty more positively than do most. People shuffled around the lobby area apprehensively, stooped, eyes on the floor. When the staff directed everyone where to go, you could not help but feel grouped according to misdeed. ("Got behind the wheel after drinking? First floor." "Ran an escort service out of a nail salon? Third floor.")

Outside the elevator on the failed-to-hold-your-marriage-together floor, my attorney awaited me. I signed papers and handed over a check. My wife arrived with her lawyer. We did not interact. We each probably did not know our tolerance level. No reason to test it.

In the front of the courtroom, with her on the left and me on the right, the judge recited her dismal lines. Our wedding vows, I have to say, were a bit more cheerful. We had to provide our verbal assent to the questions of dissolution. I tried to speak loudly and clearly, but I probably slurred and whispered. The judge tied a bow on our union with a paragraph or two, wished us well and swept us out, making way for the next couple's transition to the wrong column of marital statistics. I stayed behind for several minutes after my now ex-wife had exited. I thought as I waited: *What have we become? Newly-deads? Newly-fleds?* The coast clear, my attorney and I walked outside. She commended my steadiness and gave a sanguine statement about new beginnings, perhaps her standard language when unleashing clients into the wild.

"I wasn't exactly looking for a new beginning," I said.

"Well, you got one," she said.

I did.

On my trip home, I listened to "The Song is Over" by The Who and stopped for a doughnut, because if you cannot have a doughnut on the morning of your divorce, when can you? I then sat on my couch for hours, doing nothing. Around six in the evening, I visited my parents. My father knew what had transpired. My mother did not. I stepped into their home and stated as plainly as I could, "Mom, Dad, I got divorced today."

Not a great day, but not my saddest.

The evening I returned to my house after my ex-wife had removed all of her belongings also would not top the sadness charts. I had vacated the premises for the weekend to offer her full, unfettered access. I returned that Sunday, bracing for the worst. Maybe I would collapse in a heap at the bottom of the stairs, stunned catatonic for days until the staff from the coffee shop conducted a wellness check after I had missed a few mornings. Perhaps I frenetically would begin to paint every wall a new color, only to drop dead upon completion, like a modern-day, scaled-down, suburban John Henry. In reality, nothing. No distress as I stepped into each room, even with the knowledge she had been there hours earlier, likely for the last time. Just nothing. Maybe I had calloused up more than I had realized.

No, saddest moments tend to maneuver in a clandestine fashion, hiding in plain sight among the ordinary, lurking until our defenses relax. Exactly what happened to me.

An unremarkable Tuesday night in the fall, back when my mother still would go out in the evenings. We had dinner at a nearby restaurant, a tame sports tavern that buzzed with families after soccer practice and happy-hour coworkers not ready to head home. She enjoyed the large-screen televisions streaming in games, the multiple conversations thrumming in the background. She liked the waiters and waitresses, each one so solicitous of her. A naturally social personality, she had become even more outgoing in public settings, the illness having chipped away at her few inhibitions. She would start discussions with strangers and interact buoyantly with workers in stores. Some politely smiled. Others squinted, perplexed. A few—like the staff in that particular restaurant—spotted the malady beneath the cheer. She would greet them like family—"There he is! So good to see you!"—and talk far longer than necessary, oblivious to their other responsibilities. They would respond so graciously. Such simple human decency, but incalculable.

Over dinner, my mother and I fell into a typical exchange, covering typical topics.

"Did you know my father?" she said.

"I didn't."

"Why not?"

"He passed away before I was born."

"I didn't know that. Well, you would have liked him and he would have liked you."

"You think so?"

"Oh, sure. He would take me into the city one day each year for lunch. It was our day. He asked what I wanted to eat and one time, I said a chicken club sandwich. I didn't even know what it was. It just sounded fun. We went to three different places until we found one with a chicken club sandwich. I was so embarrassed. I didn't have to have it, but he insisted. That's the kind of guy he was. Did you know that story?"

"I didn't."

I did. She had shared it many, many times. The prior week, in fact. No advantage in undercutting her enthusiasm or, more importantly, reminding her of the infirmity.

We had not spoken of the divorce in months, not really much at all after I had broken the news and after that unpleasantness on July Fourth. I often wondered if she even remembered I once had a wife. Or if she noticed how my body composition had shifted to twenty-percent organic matter and eighty-percent stress due to unresolved questions. Not the worst development, if she did not recall, either for her or for me.

Compartmentalization. I long had associated the term with sociopaths or supercharged careerists. The practice, though, useful during this period. Intellectually, I understood my mother's illness had nothing to do with my divorce, nor did my divorce have anything to do with my mother's illness. Emotionally, though, I could have blended them together quite easily and with unfortunate results. I had to separate the two. I had to compartmentalize. Even as each chugged along on an individual track, the mechanism at the junction could malfunction and they could collide. As they did that night.

I returned with my mother to the house for a few hours. Upon my departure, we went through what had become our standard dialogue.

"Why don't you stay here?"

"I need to go to my place tonight. Maybe I'll stay here one night soon, though."

Outside on the front steps, in the brisk autumn air of burning firewood and fallen leaves, my mother hugged me goodbye, as usual. After a second or two, I pulled away, but she squeezed me more tightly. Her arms, still strong, but spindly. Her frame, dwindled inside her sagging sweater. She put her hand behind my head, at the base of my neck. Her voice cracked.

"When I think about what's happened to you, I get so damn upset. And I can't do anything to help you. I can't sleep at night."

The sadness hit like a medical emergency. A wrenching tightness across my mouth, around my throat. An eruption of pressure through my forehead, temples and eyes. My chest and stomach caved in on themselves. I could not speak. I could not say, "I'm fine, Mom." I turned away, down the stairs. I could not let her see me. Could not look at her. She called after me, "Are you okay?" I did not face her, but raised my right arm in the air and waved it. I picked up my pace to a jog, as if the energy would calm her. I got in my car and drove only a few blocks. I parked on the side of the road and sobbed.

The thoughts, a downpour all over me, without form or rhythm. Her love for her son stymied by broken faculties. The flickering realization she could not process the circumstances. In the middle of the night, her head unable to rationalize its way to a secure place, unaided by history and the possibility things could get better. Like a child waking from a nightmare, but without a parent to comfort her. Her last conscious memories of me, heartbroken and alone. Such guilt for what I had put her through.

The moment would remain with me in perpetuity, I knew then and know now. As much a part of me as my cells and tissue. From then on, whenever I would think of my mother, this recollection would shove its way to the front of my head, reminding me of her frail, final years, of the hurt she felt on my behalf. A pain so pure and undiluted and unrefined. A sorrow so big, I could not even attempt to fold it in half, then in half again, to pack away or ship off somewhere else. A sadness so dense and heavy, all else—before and after—seemed like ether.

Sitting in Sainte-Anne-de-Beaupre, I finally felt moved.

13

IF ONE DEFINES PRAYING as concentration on a problem with the hope for a resolution, yet with the underlying acceptance such a resolution likely never will materialize, then I prayed while sitting in the basilica.

My mind still worked as it did when I was a child. At a younger age, I remember observing adults in church playing out rather intense religious adherence. Kneeling with their eyes clenched so tightly the lids might have split open. Nose bridges pressed to interlaced knuckles. Or heads trained slightly upward, transfixed by the cross hanging behind the altar. Back then, thoughts ricocheted around my skull. Irrelevant thoughts. Cartoons. Toys. Side glances out the window that became full-blown stares, imagining running around and playing a game of freeze tag with friends on the church lawn. I had assumed that as I aged my methods would mature into a form resembling serious prayer. Not quite. My posture, straight. My pose, appropriately solemn. My thoughts, still occasionally irrelevant and still ricocheting around my skull. Even as I sat in the Basilica of Sainte-Anne-de-Beaupré as a (supposedly) fully developed man with a (somewhat) clear purpose, my focus shook. As I had suspected regarding all aspects of my life, I only looked like an adult.

My mother, I could picture quite well, stationed in a nearby pew on any number of her visits to Saint Anne's. I had witnessed her in the act of prayer far more often than I had any other human being. For me, she had cast the model of reverence. I certainly could not read her mind while she prayed, as she certainly could not have read mine, gratefully so. She did not know of my irrelevant thoughts. Even if she had, I doubt she would have disciplined me, nor do I think she would have been disappointed in me. She demanded respect and quiet, of course, but never did she instruct anyone how to pray. She did not stress the need to follow a script or meet some quota of recitations. She practiced a faith of comfort, with tolerance for irrelevant thoughts.

No ironclad dogma and icy dictums for my mother. No invocation of authority for authority's sake, on which some rely to defend religious traditions. The chain of her reasoning never included a link of "just because." Having said that, she maintained a practical view of the lived world, one in which, "Things just happen," certainly beyond any individual's control and without any rhyme. Some might stall on such questions as, "Why do good people suffer?" My mother did not spend much time on these issues. People— good and bad—would continue to suffer before ever unearthing a satisfactory explanation, if one even could exist. Better to direct energy and effort toward more pragmatic ends.

She did not pray to alter events or avert crises, but only for the fortitude to withstand them. More for others than for herself. More action than prayer, as well, as she administered a type of secular ministry. A close acquaintance's daughter might have struggled with addiction. My mother would arrange for counseling. A neighbor might have received a cancer diagnosis. My mother would accompany her to chemotherapy sessions. When these temporal interventions had run their course, either favorably or unfavorably, she would take these individuals to Quebec.

Saint Anne's, in many ways, represented for her the gift of faith, one given to her and one she shared with others. When I was much younger and she prepared to leave on one of her trips to Quebec, I asked her where she was going. She answered, "To visit a friend." Even at that age, I might have rolled my eyes at the loose allegory, the type a parent devises to hang close enough to honesty without having to chase after follow-up questions. As I edged into adulthood and began to recognize which of my own friendships would stand the test of years, miles and everyday distractions, I appreciated the truth in my mother's characterization of faith as a relationship. How natural for you to seek time with a friend to set yourself straight? If having to travel some distance, do the moments together not become that much more valuable? The minutes and hours in that person's company leave you more grateful, more grounded, more aware of a better self that might have dimmed from view. And when you part, you do so not into a recalibrated world, but as a recalibrated person. So, yes, my mother would drive to Canada, "To visit a friend." It is hard to argue with such a position, even for the faithless.

I could have concluded there in the assessment of my mother's faith. Tempting to do so. I had landed on a positive, if not passive and simple reading. A reading that would have sold her rather short, though. Yes, she could admit, "Things just happen." Far more often than not, she promoted the notion, "Things happen for a reason." She could alternate between the two perspectives to navigate life's choppy waters, switching between one and the other according to the current's demands, frustratingly and inconsistently so. On one occasion, "Things happen for a reason." On another, "Things just happen." Perhaps therein lies a true mystery of faith: knowing when to apply which point of view.

Somewhat easier, I suspect, to erect an existence on the foundation of "Things just happen." More dependable. Less painful. Fewer letdowns, without having to build oneself up again and again. Curious and contradictory, then, for the woman who advised, "You only get hurt when you have expectations," to have applied so much of herself to finding the reasons powering otherwise unreasonable events. I had come to understand she had no choice. It was who she was.

Again, she composed poetry. The religious spilled into the artistic. The artistic leaked into the theological. She practiced a creative faith.

Questions regarding my mother could serve as questions regarding all writers. Did she extract and interpret meaning? Or did she ascribe and inscribe meaning otherwise not present? Probably both to varying degrees. Either way or both ways, she wove everything together so exquisitely, you could not see the seams. Each setback just a plot turn in a narrative lunging toward triumph. Every success the confirmation of providence. For example, shortly after my grandmother passed away, my cousin announced her pregnancy. My mother framed the news as evidence of a glorious continuum between life and the afterlife. One less symbolically minded would have concluded that my grandmother's expiration roughly coincided with another wholly unrelated biological occurrence. A conciliatory approach could acknowledge the transmission of DNA among generations, so, therefore, a portion of my grandmother would endure, so to speak. A compromise between physics and metaphysics. Regardless, my mother's interpretation helped her manage an extraordinary loss. Why bother disagreeing with her?

I cannot deny how I often wished to inhabit a world filtered through her prism. One in which randomness would reveal itself as serendipity. One in which misunderstood beauty would break through the shell of imperfection. One in which each deficit ultimately would total a magnificent sum. I also cannot deny how this world could wear you out. Always having to stitch ordinary circumstances into a grander tapestry. Always having to play a role in an ongoing meta-drama. Always having to locate meaning, when, well, "Things just happen." Sometimes you do not do well on a test in school. Sometimes you have a bad day or a string of bad days. Sometimes husbands and wives just get divorced. None of it calls for an aesthetic-existential justification, since none of it signifies very much at all. "Things just happen."

At the basilica, simmering, I attempted to cool off. I placed my palms flat on the glassy wood seat and clasped my fingers around the smooth, sloping end. "Things just happen" dines at the same holiday table as, "It is what it is." I should not have overlooked one as I flared in defense of the other. Children do not respond as parents wish. Parents do not respond as children wish. From infant to elder, the back-and-forth disappointment continues until parent or child can accept the other as a flawed, autonomous individual. Maturity and resignation grow to resemble one another, particularly when it comes to family. Unfair to my mother, then, to have expected her to adjust style and outlook to meet my vacillating expectations. Especially unfair, since as my mind wandered here and there while supposedly in prayer, she would not have scolded me. A little meandering, she trusted, ultimately would lead me to a worthwhile destination. Whether intentional or accidental, her method obviously had succeeded. After years and years of irrelevant thoughts, there I found myself, at Saint Anne's, just like my mother.

If she had retained more of herself at the time I had disclosed to her the conclusion of my marriage, I believe she soon after would have traveled to Quebec to pray for me. Not to undo the dissolution with a rabbit-out-of-a-hat reconciliation, but to guide me into an unknowable future. I took the trip she could not.

A sensation then overcame me, the harsh deflation when you remember how you neglected to pack an essential item, like a passport, or forgotten a critical errand, like paying your taxes. Part admonition. Part helplessness. I had ignored something so obvious. My mother also would have made another visit to Saint Anne's. One for herself.

If she had suffered a different ailment, one that had attacked her body more than her mind, she would have driven to Canada. Before the altar, she would not have wailed or moaned. Certainly not. Yes, as noted, none of us truly know the silent prayers of another, but my mother always had assured me not to worry at her passing. She believed the faith that had governed her days would prepare her to take a next step. Of course, she likely had anticipated a swifter strike, one with a conscious surrender to a final passage, not a slow, deliberate deterioration.

How would my mother have prayed for herself?

Please give me strength. Please give strength to those around me. Please let them know they are loved.

In truth, can the faithful or the faithless ever ask for more?

And when my mother had said her final prayer and exited through the doors of the basilica one last time, stepping away from safety into a series of punishing days, which perspective would she have carried with her? "Things just happen"? Or "Things happen for a reason"? The answer, I do not know. Again, perhaps therein lies a true mystery of faith: knowing when to apply which point of view.

Which perspective would I carry with me when I would leave the church? Awaited in the coming years by hospital stays and twenty-four care and sepsis and intravenous hydration, I would slouch into a future in which, "Things just happen." More dependable. Less painful. Fewer letdowns. Perhaps less courageous and creative, as well.

If I could barricade myself within fatalism as we managed a disease with no cure, others chose not to do so, specifically my father. My brothers and I individually had made our peace with the illness. We had accepted the unrelenting progression toward an inevitable conclusion, whether an infection her system could not stare down or the drawn-out deprivation of her metabolic functions. Not my father. He clutched unyieldingly the idea, "Things happen for a reason."

He wrestled with the question, "How could this happen to her?" He preserved the logical relationship between cause and effect, because when an effect has a cause, the situation stands a greater chance of reversal. Stated more simply, in his mind, my mother could get better. What initially appeared as willful ignorance, I began to understand as supreme faith. A faith beyond institutions and rites and rituals. Never directly stated to anyone, but fully demonstrated in his dedication: "One person must believe she will improve. I promised to be that person. I will keep my promise."

With my mother robbed of the comfort granted by her own faith, my father filled the void with his personal devotion. The preparation of each meal. The daily provision of her favorite beverage (green tea latte). Shopping for clothes to cover her diminishing frame in dignity. The ongoing search for stimulation—photo albums, clippings of articles she had written, visits with friends—something that might return her to the self that receded farther and farther from view. And, yes, the absorption of her hostility.

"You took away my car!"

"I never said that!"

"Why do you keep me in this place?"

The disease lays bare fear's rather elementary evolution into anger. My mother sat terrified almost every minute. Her terror turned into rage blasted at the nearest target: my father. He took it without a word.

"I'm fine. The poor woman is in pain," he would say through hollowed cheeks, his blood pressure spiking, his eyes sinking more deeply into his head.

My father denied himself the space afforded by pure intellectual analysis. He instead chose to rise and fall with each good and bad day. He would search for a pattern in the splotchy, chaotic mural painted by her sickness. He would suffer through her worst moments. During her better moments, he would soar, only to crash back to reality almost immediately. He paid a price for his faith, over and over again, without ever counting the cost.

14

"DO YOU HAVE ANYONE?"

"What do you mean?"

"You know. Anyone. Anyone else."

"No, not anymore. I did once."

"I didn't know that."

"I thought you did."

"No, I didn't."

"I'm mistaken, then. I'm sorry."

"Maybe you should get someone."

"Maybe. Not now, though."

15

"THE GROOM'S PREVIOUS MARRIAGE ENDED IN DIVORCE."

I discovered some of my horribly judgmental tendencies while sitting on a park bench, reading these words. On Sunday mornings, I drove two towns away from my own to limit the possibility of seeing anyone I might know while I tried to relax for a few hours. Not that I knew many people. I resided in my town more so than lived there. At a certain age, without children and the attendant school events and activities to thread you into the community, you are a bit of a loose strand. Get pulled out and the fabric does not pinch. You shop in stores and visit the post office to get stamps every so often. At most, you deal with municipal officials over permits for home improvements. I had developed some nice friendships with baristas at the coffee shop and the woman at the dry cleaner and the employees at the pharmacy. Nothing quite like the ties my brothers and sisters-in-law knotted with their fellow parents during practices and concerts and birthday parties.

Loose strand though I might have been, I still did not wish to risk seeing anyone or, for that matter, being seen.

On Sundays, two towns away, I bought my drink at a different shop, somewhat ashamed by stepping out on my weekly coffee spouses for a quick dalliance. I crossed the street to the park and chose one of the two benches along the bank of the brook. I preferred the wooden one shaded by the tree instead of the metal one out in the open, the surface of which heated up uncomfortably in the slightest sunlight. (Why the planners had not switched the positioning of the two, I do not know.) Once settled, I read the newspaper, cover-to-cover, even the sections that normally did not interest me. Real estate. Opinion. Lifestyle. I consumed almost anything to prolong the minutes, a brief vacation from the racket in my head.

I even skimmed the wedding announcements, a masochistic practice, some might note. The entries brought about no emotional-psychological response. Comforting, in fact, as if a form of exposure therapy. I neither criticized the couples—*They'll see!*—nor did I envy them. The divorce had not darkened my overall opinion of marriage, which surprised those around me. Admittedly, both personal history and more general longitudinal data should have let a little air out of my tires. But no. This same overly positive, somewhat oblivious attitude had enabled me to exist within my own marriage without pinpointing the fissures and crevices. For years and years, I had been guilty of an obnoxious brand of nuptial exceptionalism, as if to say, "I know relationships have difficulties, but I have it figured out." I clearly did not have it figured out.

"The groom's previous marriage ended in divorce."

This, the last sentence in one announcement I read that Sunday, sitting on that bench. Sort of jarring. A tour through the happy details—how the couple met, bridal-party composition, honeymoon location—then whacked by a reminder of the institution's fragility. Just ask the groom. Why not write, "The bride claimed her slightly used husband on the secondary market"?

At first, indignation over the newspaper forcing the line into the article. Was it really necessary? Why contaminate pleasantness with unpleasantness? ("Places everyone. This guy's wedding ... Take two. Roll 'em!") Similar resentment gurgled up when I had to fill out paperwork at a doctor's office, which asked me to list my status as single, married or divorced. Well, if I am divorced, I am single, so why the hell must I disclose that I once was married? Actually, such events might affect one's health, so I understand why medical professionals would want to know, however irksome.

I again read the sentence: "The groom's previous marriage ended in divorce."

I then imagined what I would have thought upon seeing that line months and months earlier, back when I floated inside my own matrimonial bubble, believing it never could burst.

I would have judged.

I would have speculated that the fractured couple had entered into the marriage too hastily, too blindly, without an appreciation of the required commitment.

I would have questioned when they had measured the results no longer worth the effort, when they started doing less and expecting more, when they began to keep score. What had they taken for granted about one another, taken for granted about the relationship? I would have wondered if either ever should have gotten married in the first place. The lifestyle does not suit everyone, with cultural and societal insistence continuously ramming square pegs into round holes. Essentially, I would have judged according to standards I assumed I had met, not aware of the sweat pouring down my face from having flown so closely and smugly to the sun.

I would have judged as harshly as others likely judged me. At least, others judged me harshly in my own mind, which contains an awful capacity to generate and amplify grievances. Even so, quite a bit of judgment out there, I learned.

Gossipy rainclouds seemed to follow me. One day, after an exchange with an acquaintance I gladly would have avoided if we had not almost physically crashed into one another on the sidewalk, she did not even wait for me to travel beyond earshot to say to her companion, "You know he got divorced, right? I heard—" I managed to tune her out. I might have taken greater offense, if this person possessed any talent other than making miserable everyone with whom she would come in contact. Indicative, nevertheless, of the nastiness that can trail a person.

Nothing short of a sin, my divorce to some. Many of the religiously preoccupied consider marriage a sacrament, an indissoluble bond forged before God. Whether one agrees or disagrees with such a point of view, to return to an earlier, non-religious tenet, "Things just happen." What kind of things? None of anyone's business. The pious might determine that you just quit when the going got tough. You might argue, "I did my best," only to receive a pursed-mouth, cross-eyed reply, "If you think so." They might recite some banality like, "Obedience is the ultimate sacrifice." By all means, sacrifice away for both of us. Those who wield religion like a blade or bludgeon merit no explanation. Playing along with their sanctimony, I suspect the judgmental place themselves far closer to the front of the Damnation Line than do divorcees. So, enjoy.

Less overt, more insidious than the self-righteous squadron, certain individuals exploited the divorce as the entry point through which to conduct more comprehensive and entirely irrelevant judgment. The divorce, to them, a break in the character dam, failure spilling out and washing over every region of life. Second-guess this guy as much as you wish about anything you like—movie recommendations, whether to bring a coat on a cold day, etc.—because he so severely has erred.

Judgment also presented itself as a type forensic analysis. When others—not close friends—asked about my divorce and I gave as brief a summary as possible, they often reflexively supplied appraisals.

"It sounds like you might have been too young."

"It seems like you both were busy with your own careers."

"You probably grew apart."

"Marriage is tough."

I understand that by alluding to external factors, these individuals attempted to absolve me of personal responsibility. But they were not there. No one was. No one knows what happened and did not happen. No one has a clear window into your relationship. No one knows anything about your marriage, just as I did not know anything about how "The groom's previous marriage ended in divorce." The members of that former couple had every right to tell me to go to hell.

Aside from a few occasions here and there, people judged me less severely than I had judged others, less severely than I judged myself. And I judged myself quite severely. When I did, I needed compassion, which I thankfully received.

I again read the last line of the announcement: "The groom's previous marriage ended in divorce."

The sentence made me angry, but fear, as noted, rests directly beneath anger. In that Sunday newspaper, a reminder of one of my greatest, perhaps most irrational fears from the earliest days of my divorce.

Foremost, I should acknowledge that becoming involved with another person at first seemed like an impossibility. Just not interested. Despite my reluctance, I still wished to preserve the theoretical possibility. I had to maintain the contingency that I might want to get married again one day. Or I might not. Nothing gained by removing any eventuality from the table. (Again, in theory.) A mistake, I had concluded, to dictate either that a new life in no way would simulate my earlier one or that I absolutely had to re-create the conditions of my prior existence. Committing to either direction could lead me nowhere fulfilling. "Let the chips fall where they may" and all.

Before I had reasoned my way to that mindset, cataclysmic notions bounced around my head: *I am damaged. I am tainted. What parent ever would want his or her daughter to date me?*

A neo-medieval assessment not entirely unlike the fire-and-brimstone kindled by the divorce-equals-damnation sect. But I thought emotionally, not clearly in those early days. My mind eventually settled, yet the concern continued, albeit to less of an extreme. Should I ever find myself in a relationship, I could hear that woman's family and friends confiding in one another, "He certainly seems nice, but he is divorced. Do we really know what happened?" An objectively fair point, one with which I would have to contend. Preposterous to worry as I did, some counseled, but it is hard not to let certain irrationalities embed too deeply.

And, yes, judgment had embedded too deeply into my being. Judgment of self, primarily, as if a self-administered inoculation against the worst others could do to me. ("Move along. Nothing to judge here. This one already pulverized himself into dust.") Even as friends attempted to set me up on dates and even as I recognized the many examples of those who had moved on without others giving it a second thought, my head still corkscrewed in destructive directions.

"The groom's previous marriage ended in divorce."

One day, I would let that one go. Just not on that Sunday morning, as I sat on the bench by the brook.

16

WHEN YOU ENTER THE Basilica of Sainte-Anne-de-Beaupre, one feature arrests you: climbing up the marble pillars, row-upon-row of crutches and canes and walkers abandoned by those who limped in and strode out. A child might label the visual either awesome or terrifying. A thin line—if any line at all—separates the sacred from the scary. Not unlike how I felt in religious settings or during religious ceremonies when much younger, thinking: *This is weird and I'm uncomfortable, but the teacher insists I have to be here and I don't want to get in trouble, so I'll go along with it.* I would look at the other children, their hands pressed together and fingers in perfect rows, voices loud and strong above liturgical music and through prayer recitation, asking myself: *Do they not think this is weird? Are they not uncomfortable? Are they just trying to get on the teacher's good side? Is something wrong with me?*

In any event, the crutches and canes and walkers adorning the basilica convey no subtext, only straight, clear text: "Miracles happen here." One could coarsen the message with an auto-showroom sales pitch: "And you, too, could get your very own miracle if you come in today."

The subject of miracles likely sorts a person into one of two groups. Some outright deny the possibility due to science or empiricism. Of course, the same skeptics might welcome one under the right conditions. Others see miracles far too frequently, in last-second three-pointers by favorite teams or in high marks on tests earned without the benefit of preparation. In my case, I split the difference: I would accept a miracle if presented, but I would not necessarily argue on behalf of its right to exist. Why completely reject a concept I might one day need? My funhouse-mirror interpretation of Pascal's Wager. My aversion to the miraculous predicated less on the theological and more on the aesthetic. A little too saccharine for my taste, attributing a positive outcome to heavenly intercession. A careless storytelling device, as well, with the arbitrary threads of chance and suffering and success tied together too neatly.

Entirely hypocritical of me to take such a position, especially as I sat in that church pew. My situation certainly did not call for a miracle. Asking for one would be excessive, a chainsaw to a sheet of paper when scissors would suffice.

I do not know if I believe in miracles.

I do know that on my worst days, the phone would ring at the right time.

Or a message would appear on my phone.

Or someone would invite me to lunch.

These acts, guided not by a divine hand, but rather by kindness and friendship.

I remember each of them. Every conversation. Every note. Every secondary inquiry into my well-being. ("'So-and-so' asked how you were holding up.") Each kept me upright, day-by-day.

I heard from those with whom I had stayed in continuous communication, of course. The former coworker who dropped everything on the spot to meet and talk me through a difficult afternoon. ("Stop your nonsense.") A colleague stationed in Nairobi who awoke at three in the morning her time, just so she could call me in the evening in my time zone. The friend from the West Coast, who—on a quick visit east—ducked out of a family gathering for an hour to have a drink with me.

Somewhat unexpectedly, those with whom I had lost touch also reached out. The news had trickled to a buddy from high school, as well as two friends from my study-abroad program in college. They penned multiple encouraging messages, volunteered their homes if I ever just had to get out of town for a few days. We eased effortlessly back into our banter, conversations resumed as if paused only days earlier, not years. We mocked one another's eccentricities, the way only someone who knew you in your formative years can. All a healthy reminder: *You did know what it was like to be happy before.*

These semi-long-lost companions also answered for me an important question: As the primacy of adult relationships and obligations deprioritizes those from our past—harmlessly and unintentionally so—do these individuals hold grudges? No, not them. Once their friend, always their friend, they showed me.

While those first communications meant a great deal, even more worthwhile were the follow-ups. Fairly consistently, out of nowhere, people contacted me.

"How are you?"

"Anything you need?"

"You hanging in?"

During the November-to-December holiday season, everyone flocked to me, so much so and with such coordination, I wondered if someone had engineered a kindhearted collusion. ("Everybody know the plan? Synchronize your watches and meet back here at the beginning of January.") Invitations to parties. Inclusion in tree selections and the like. A visit to the garden center that annually transforms its interior into a garish, Christmas-tableau fever dream, a two-dollar tour past window-after-window of Santa-suited cartoon characters in jolly copyright infringement. A greater influx of cards filled my mailbox, with only a few people having cut me from their lists. One cousin scribbled next to the photo of her family posed in matching red-and-green sweaters, "Sorry to hear about your divorce. Merry Christmas!" If she had intended to make me laugh out loud while alone in my kitchen, she succeeded.

To a person, my friends invested emotionally in my story, a virtual, rabid mob gathering with pitchforks and torches, one I had to corral and calm. ("I'm going to need everyone to settle down. No one is doing anything he or she will regret. We don't want to have to call the National Guard.") No real threat. They only wanted me to know they had my back. They took up the fight for a little while, so I could devote less attention to reasoning through a heartrending enigma and more to recuperating.

Most restoratively, people just listened. Over and over again, I unloaded inanity and fright and panic and senselessness. They took every scrap. Somehow, my family, friends and I had struck a silent bargain with one another. I never would say, "You don't understand," provided they never would advise, "You really should …" We faithfully adhered to these terms, although I suspect doing so presented challenges for them. I likely drove them a little crazy. My failure—or refusal—to absorb logic probably irritated them more than they ever would have admitted to me. Who knows? Maybe they had side discussions with one another in which they commiserated, "The guy just won't let go." They were more than entitled to a little venting.

But I did hear them, even if it appeared I did not. I heard every single word. A variety of interpretations and perspectives came my way. Some funny. ("One day, a woman will want to stay in the country badly enough that she will agree to marry you.") Some blunt. ("She's gone. Move on.") Some sensitive. ("Don't be so hard on yourself.") Some heartwarming. ("She might have known you better, but I've known you longer, so I can tell you to not believe the worst.") All of them, very much needed.

With the talking finished, people then tried to get me out of the house.

My parents gave me everything in life, but no gift greater than my siblings. Just when I thought I might have matured beyond the big brother-little brother dynamic, I again found myself very much within the ageless framework, gratefully so. Just as they did when we had grown-up together, my brothers took care of me, protected me, let me tag along. Like clockwork, I heard from each of them every single day. My sisters-in-law—among my fiercest defenders—always made room for me, if I needed to drop-by to unwind in a place beyond the all-too familiar walls of my house.

Their children, they qualify as miracles to me. Not nearly old enough to understand my predicament, they nevertheless tuned into my unique sadness. They drew me pictures. They accompanied me on walks through the reservation. They roped me into games of Monopoly that strayed comically far from the rules. They insisted on hanging a stocking with my name above the fireplace in their home at Christmas. All a healthy reminder: *You will know what it is like to be happy afterward.*

Friends had me over for dinner and included me in social gatherings, even if I just hovered on the periphery.

During that first summer, I remember how three separate individuals asked me to see the same movie. The funniest film in the theaters at the time, it might cheer me up, each person expected. I went all three times, never disclosing to the latter two how I already had caught it. I laughed just as hard at every viewing. Most of all, I recall each person's thoughtfulness.

"My girlfriend can't make the Crosby, Stills and Nash concert," another friend said in the autumn. "Why don't you join me?"

I still suspect his girlfriend absolutely could have attended the concert, but he wanted me to feel as if I were doing him a favor. In a humorous aside we will reference *ad infinitum*, at the show, I ran into someone I sort-of recognized through work. Rather than cordially approach him, I pointed and shouted, "I know you." My friend put his arm around me and said, "We need to work on your social skills." Too much time on my own had rusted me up a little.

My one friend, upon whose place of work I had descended on the first day of the divorce, went on a first-ballot, Hall-of-Fame tear. When he said, "We're going to get through this," I believed him, yes, but I also understood the natural limitations. People, after all, have lives to lead. Damn, if he did not keep his word.

Every Monday evening, he came to my house to watch football. When the season ended, we searched for a substitute and somehow landed on professional wrestling. I had abandoned the "sport" right before

I had entered high school, a hobby I could not quite rationalize to members of the opposite sex. Suddenly, decades later, when I had expected to chart my calendar according to school vacations, I instead marked my time by wrestling pay-per-views. I could have (should have) stopped at any point, but I had grown to love those hours. The two of us volleying theories about the basketball season. The crazy observations to get the other person to laugh. We even conceived of a panel show, which would feature two mainstream, expert guests, along with a retired or current professional wrestler as the third guest.

"The topic," I announced, "is race relations in twenty-first century America."

"That's easy," he replied. "Cornel West, Toni Morrison and Booker-T."

"Try this one," he countered. "The topic is religion's waning influence in the marketplace of rapid technological advancement."

"Marilynne Robinson, Rick Warren and the Undertaker," I answered.

Another of my closest friends, who lived several states away, called me regularly for check-ins and pep talks, usually delivering his candid, hysterical philosophy. On my first birthday following the divorce, he traveled to spend the weekend with me. He planned stops at a number of sites throughout the city, dragging around my listless frame like a stuffed animal he had just won at a carnival booth. He reserved for us a table at a restaurant recommended by some upscale publication. At dinner, he charmed the staff into supplying an oversized marshmallow with a single candle. No singing, I insisted, a relief to all.

"Make a wish, buddy," he said.

As I blew out the flame, I did not wish for the upcoming year to look different from the previous months. I just thought to myself: *This isn't so bad.*

When I reflect on the divorce, my mind turns to these experiences. I do not dwell too long on the loneliness and loss. No, I think of the generosity. And I am more grateful than I ever could express.

As the months passed and I seemed to be managing the situation, some asked, "How have you gotten through it?" They (falsely) attributed to me resilience or grit. No, none of that. My family and friends got me through it, as mawkish as that might read. I cannot think of a more accurate way in which to capture what took place. In getting me through it, they also taught me a lesson, one I had overlooked or taken for granted when others around me had encountered similar difficulties.

I try to resist boiling life down to epigrams. (Emphasis on *try*.) Too cute. Too orderly. Reality, a little too complicated, a bit too diverse, with far too much beyond our control. I doubt anyone ever will settle conclusively the what's-it-all-about debate. Nor should we want the debate to end, its ongoing byproducts too enjoyable, too enriching. But because it is so complicated and diverse and beyond our control, with all of us helpless before the vicissitudes, I think our ultimate value lies in being there for one another, regardless of the form taken by the "being there." As far as I can determine—whatever you believe or do not believe—we serve no greater purpose.

17

ULTIMATELY, I FOUND MY NEW ROUTINE.

Through trial and error, I discovered the sequence of movements and tasks that formed into habits, which enabled me to proceed with the right proportion of mindless-action-to-reflection. If thinking held incendiary properties, I would have self-combusted multiple times a day during those early months. The more room and oxygen allowed for my thoughts, the greater the personal hazard. I had to contain the fire without completely stomping out the flame. After all, I still had work to do. Shutting down all contemplation would have performed a disservice. Nevertheless, I had to occupy myself with fairly thoughtless activities.

Weekdays were easy, so much of the time already not my own. Awake around five in the morning, on the train by six-thirty, into the office. Back on the train, home by seven-thirty, then maybe to the gym, unless too tired or too lazy. Home by nine-thirty, with only about ninety minutes or so before trying to fall asleep.

Weekends required more effort. Friday nights, I had dinner with my parents. I would pick up the meal on the way to their house or my father and I would drive together to retrieve it. My mother would follow her own routine by carefully laying out the placemats and silverware for the three of us. During basketball season, we would watch a game. I would head home at halftime, then catch the final two quarters before going to bed.

I established one rule for Saturday: out the door. Not long after waking up, I had to remove myself from the house as soon as possible. If not, thirty minutes could balloon into three hours, then five hours, the day swallowed up by itself.

If the weather permitted, I would walk in the nearby reservation, sometimes for hours. Week after week after week, my steps pounded down the trail to the lake, then up the dusty hill, across the shallow brook, through the dense, buggy woods and out into the open field. Almost always the same route. What changed, over the months, were the songs piping through my headphones. My soundtrack eventually had to expand. You only can ingest so much sap and melancholy before the diet leaves you somewhat ill. For example, I once attended a charity fundraiser in which professional actors belted show-stopping song after show-stopping song from Broadway musicals. By the end, I felt as if I had stumbled away from an airplane crash. A listener requires diversity, some adjustments in tempo and tone. As grateful as I always would be to the likes of Millie Jackson and David Gray, I had to include some new artists in the rotation.

Instead of playing "She's Gone" by Tavares or the Tower of Power's "So Very Hard to Go" on a loop, I mixed in the spirited defiance of Honey Cone's "One Monkey Don't Stop No Show" and the playful pursuit of Clarence Carter's "Looking for a Fox." Out with Joe Cocker's "Bye Bye Blackbird" and in with "Break It Down Again" by Tears for Fears.

On Saturday evenings, I almost always went to the movies, either with friends or by myself. According to my calculation, I had seen thirty-one films alone since my marriage had ended. Quantity over quality, certainly. I would have watched almost anything for the communal experience of sitting in a theater with human beings. I could be among others without having to associate with them, about all I could manage. Isolated socialization or socialized isolation, however trained experts might describe the practice. When the credits rolled—the film either good or bad—I took with me a sense of accomplishment. I had done something, however passive and insignificant.

On Sunday mornings, in warmer weather, I would sit on the park bench and read. Before visiting my mother for our outing, I sometimes would watch the soccer and softball games of my brothers' children. I became a fixture on the sidelines, so much so, the other parents assumed my own son or daughter participated. I usually concluded the weekend over dinner with family members, then back home, staring ahead at another identical seven days.

Someone joked that I had fashioned myself into the easiest person in the world to track. Just look at the clock and you would know exactly where to locate me. A comforting notion for my family.

As for a number of my friends, they considered my schedule really, really boring. These individuals had encouraged me to morph into a reckless twentysomething, like a science-fiction character sent back in time, equipped with slightly higher earnings, an additional decade of insight and little to lose. They envisioned my Tuesday evenings in swanky bars and Thursday nights on a series of first dates with women so young they had no clue the globe once had housed two Germanies. Weekends by the beach or in Monte Carlo, as if Sammy Davis Jr. and Dean Martin had substituted me for Peter Lawford. To the disappointment and confoundment of some, I actually became more like an elderly widower, stopping just short of reading magazines in the library, joining a bingo league and enrolling in a program in which high-school students visit me to earn community-service credits.

Routines generally add a higher degree of efficiency. My routine purposely made my existence less efficient. Rather than trying to kill multiple birds with a single stone, I viewed my days as vast aviaries in which birds could thrive well beyond their projected life expectancies. I would stretch out my errands. Instead of completing an online purchase, I thought: *I will just go to the store to get it.* At the supermarket, I could have bought enough for the week in one visit, but I instead packed into my handheld basket enough items for only a few days, as I wished to return at least two more times from Sunday to Saturday. I did not call to ask if the hardware store seven towns away carried the replacement igniter for my parents' grill. I traveled there. When the clerk informed me he did not keep it in stock, I sighed with relief. I would have one more thing to do the next day.

Useful. I just wanted to feel useful, to help the world around me inch forward in the smallest of increments. I genuinely enjoyed modest tasks. Picking up a cake for my niece's birthday. Walking the dog for an out-of-town friend. Helping a neighbor lift a piece of furniture and carry it to the basement. Trivial, but tangible achievements. Hard to elevate the work to the heights of purpose. More like paying rent for the room I took up on earth.

The satisfaction I derived from not much at all concerned others, I could see. Those close to me could remember when I had aspired to more, like having a family of my own, pouring myself completely into another, rather than in teaspoons. So much smaller, my life seemed. But I was happy. A form of happiness that appeared compromised to many who loved me. I sensed their worry that I would grow too comfortable with this cropped lifestyle. That I would give up on having more. That I would accept spending my time alone, until one day, being alone would have hardened like concrete.

Loneliness unavoidably pushed its way into my routine. I treated it like a temporary visitor, one I begrudgingly had to lodge. ("Listen, I know I have to let you stay with me for now, but the first second you can go, you are out of here. Deal?") The longer I put up with the loneliness, the more at home it became. ("That's loneliness. It lives here now.")

My loneliness lingered like a low-grade fever that would spike when aggravated by an external factor. Like when I took my first flight after the divorce. By the security screening, I fumbled with my passport and wallet. By habit, I turned to my right, expecting to see my wife. We had developed the type of system spouses do, in which I would hold her items while she gathered herself, after which she would do the same for me. I now had to get by on my own. Easy enough, but a slap-in-the-face reminder of my solitary status. As I walked down the terminal to my gate, I felt as though the loneliness pumped through the HVAC system, chilling right through me. I thought: *I am by myself. No one is waiting for me on the other end. No one is waiting for me when I return. If the plane crashes, whom will they notify? Should I hand a note with the name and number of a family member to the airline employee at the counter?*

The loneliness also intensified as my mother's health declined. In the past, if I had noticed a troubling new sign in her condition, I might have reviewed it with my wife. What stage had she reached? What would come next? No longer. Yes, I would call my brothers to talk about how we might respond. Those conversations naturally ended and, once off the phone, I had to face reality: *I am going to go through this alone.* Not what I had expected, certainly. The way it was, though. Luckier than many, I would have others to support me. Just not the one person I had believed would be there with me. A selfish concern, of course, considering what my parents had to endure.

As jealously as loneliness hoarded my time, its more expansive cousin also commandeered part of my routine: sadness.

Sadness can be a narcotic. Not at first. More like an infection you want to rid from your system. Eventually, your body develops a tolerance to the sadness. Then, a reliance on it, perhaps even an addiction. Certainty amidst the uncertain: *I know how to feel sad.* Something entirely unrelated would go wrong, like a mishap at work, and I could calm myself with the prospect of slipping into sadness. The woe-is-me cocktail would enter the bloodstream, clouding all of life into a haze. Dangerous, really. And lazy. Scapegoating the divorce for every slight or failure or imperfection could lead me only to bitterness. I had to resist, which I did, but not always. I would fall off the sadness wagon and indulge every now and then.

Despite the tempting sadness and the loitering loneliness, my routine had staved off a complete depression. Until my routine began to depress me.

18

EARLY ONE THURSDAY EVENING in the middle of May, I received a call from a friend. He had planned to attend a concert that night with his cousin, who canceled at the last minute. An extra ticket had become available. Mine, if I wanted it.

At one point in time, I would have outright declined. Too wedded to my regimen. Too daunted by the prospect of traveling to and from the venue. Not quite in the mood. Perhaps still tethered by an illusory obligation to a family that did not exist.

"One point in time" referred to only minutes before I had answered the phone and spoken with this friend. I already had settled into the groove through which Thursday would flow uneventfully into Friday. In the few-second pause after he had issued the invitation, I remembered how every Monday morning, I would promise myself, *This week will be different,* only for Friday to end without any meaningful deviations from the batch of prior weeks. Through my mind flashed a jumble of self-help bromides about habit and outcomes and change and saying "yes" more than "no."

"Why not?" I said. "I'll see you there."

Getting dressed for an impromptu concert does not deserve much thought from a grown man, unless, of course, he were scheduled to take the stage, which I was not. My wardrobe admittedly had undergone adjustments since the conclusion of my marriage. If more knowledgeable in the fields of entomology or zoology, I would call on an analogy about an insect or an animal shedding its exterior in crisis, only to adopt a stronger, more resplendent shell or coat. Not exactly, but also not completely off base. I suspect at least one chapter in the unwritten Starting Over manual addresses clothing. Revamping attire makes such intuitive, best-foot-forward, fresh-start sense, the practice does not require much explanation, but it should demand a higher degree of self-awareness than many apply. Experimentation with various colors and styles and fits can maroon a person on the Isle of Age Inappropriateness without a soul brave enough to launch a rescue. ("I say this with love: You look like a past-his-prime, third-tier male escort.") I had aspired to a somewhat more modern look that avoided items from the Just Got Divorced collection. I had no idea if I succeeded.

Finally in my car, I drove west almost in a straight line from my driveway, aiming just across the Pennsylvania border. I still felt as if I should ask permission regarding how I spent my time. Not from my former wife necessarily or even my parents. Not really permission, if accurate. I think I only wished for another person to know my whereabouts, for someone to have even a passing interest in my transitions from Point A to Point B and back to Point A. Again, complete freedom left me a little more alone, a little sad. On such occasions, I would reach out in transit to family members or friends with a Trojan-Horse excuse—"Did you want me to help you move those items out of your shed this weekend?"—from which I would spring the actual reason for my communication—"What am I doing? Believe it or not, I am on my way to a concert."

The highway met the sky at a soft crease. If the scene rotated ninety degrees clockwise, I would have fallen into an inviting blue pool, frothy white at the edges, heated by an orange center. Gladly so. Spring nights always swirled together nostalgia and anticipation. Transported to childhood, with homework finished and baseball practice over, enough daylight still around for more. More time outside. More chances for fun. Each lengthier day brought the promise of even more. Later bedtimes, the approaching summer schedule upending the need for structure. Conversations turning to upcoming, lazy weeks not bound by obligation. In the car, on the road to that concert, another spring night and the sense of more. Maybe more concerts. More walks into town to have a drink and watch the game. More something.

At the site, neon-vested parking attendants swung their arms in broad propeller motions to direct cars to spaces. A violet dusk surrounded the arena as the crowd funneled inside. Fizzy teenagers on their first outings. Younger parents rejoicing in the escape of their date nights. Pockets of twentysomethings obnoxiously challenging one another's fealty to the band as measured by the number shows taken in. ("Four? That's nothing. Try nine!") I seemed to straddle the third- and fourth-highest quartiles of the age demographic, although I never possessed much skill with guessing others' ages or placing mine in relation to theirs. None of which prevented me from admitting to myself an unavoidable fact: *I am getting older.*

My friend and I joined the majority of the audience in the general-admission, standing-room pit circled by a raftered balcony. The house lights down, screams and howls greeted the band. In the ambient mist, some danced around, others swayed, while many kept the beat with jutting chins, hands in their pockets. Relatively still throughout, I soaked in the spectacle by proxy. If nothing else, the experience was more diverting than my typical Thursday night. My week was different.

Finally home after eleven, a foreign electricity ran through my body. I could not just flip an "off" switch. I had to let the current flicker out and die. A pleasant change, to be kept awake by frisson, not apprehension. I sat on the couch and turned on the NBA playoffs from the West Coast, only in the second quarter. In high school, I sometimes would stay up on weeknights to see the late games, a small present to myself for which I later paid with fogginess and inattention during the next day's classes. On this night, I assured myself I would watch only until halftime, which became the third quarter and then …

The metallic growl of cans tugged by garbage collectors outside my house woke me around six in the morning. A fast, deep where-am-I breath punched into my lungs. Sitting up, hunched with elbows on my knees, cheekbones in my palms, I assessed the situation: impulsive concert across state lines, head dazed from speakers and strobes, still in my clothes, shirt suffused with splashed alcohol and crowd sweat, passed out downstairs during basketball. I wondered: *How did this become my life?*

I then considered what I once believed I would be doing on such a morning, the alternate-reality reel that almost came to play. Maybe helping children get ready for school. Perhaps making plans to meet my wife somewhere after work. Reviewing some calendar attached to the refrigerator to see what practice or birthday party awaited me during the weekend.

I paused for a second as a smile—as if from outside myself—slyly made its way up the left side of my face. I huffed a quick, muffled laugh. I wondered: *How did this become my life?*

19

IN THE FINAL DAYS OF AUGUST before I entered the eighth grade, my mother took me away for a short trip. My brothers already had gone off to college, so she might have hoped to smooth the transition into my role as the only child in the house. She also might have just wanted to go somewhere, which she always welcomed. You did not have to ask her twice about jumping in the car. The farther away the destination, the better.

"We're on an adventure," she would say.

I enjoyed American history, so my mother planned a drive to Virginia to tour Monticello, Montpellier and Ash Lawn, the respective homes of Thomas Jefferson, James Madison and James Monroe. The more deeply we wound into the state, the angrier the temperature swelled. The summer roared before having to relent to autumn. Step outside and a thin layer of dry, tan dirt instantly affixed to the back of your sweaty calves, to the inside of your elbow bend. In the canvas-topped Oldsmobile, cool and comfortable. My mother opened the windows a little, welcoming in breezes that skimmed lush lawns and whisked through trees, larger and greener than those planted near our home.

"Why don't you put on some of your music?" she said.

She might have set a trap, the way a parent can investigate a child's musical taste to determine if the artists of choice subliminally recruit underage legions to advance the cause of Satan or gang leaders. Doubtful my mother would resort to such a tactic, I still played it safe. I put in the cassette of Frank Sinatra's *Academy Award Winners*. (Yes, at twelve years old, I owned a cassette of Frank Sinatra's *Academy Award Winners*. Months earlier, on a Saturday night with my parents, I watched public television broadcast *That's Entertainment*, Metro-Goldwyn-Mayer's compilation of clips from the heyday of musicals. After seeing Frank Sinatra and Bing Crosby belt out "Well, Did You Evah" from *High Society*, I hunted for a recording. I searched bin after bin in every music store. I finally settled for Frank Sinatra's solo covers of a number of other songs from films.)

The scene imprinted itself like a multi-dimensional postcard. Timeless music. Bright sunshine. Air fragrant with local flora. Moods lifted and lightened by transport away from homebound responsibilities and toward the yet-to-be-experienced. My mother knew every song. She hummed along, which ordinarily might have irritated me, but did not then. When "All the Way" floated through the speakers, she shared how she had sung it for my father at their engagement party, which I had not known and might never have heard, if not for that visit to Virginia.

She would carry that postcard with her for the rest of her days, frequently referencing the trip throughout my teenage years, into my late-twenties and even into my thirties. Some element would trigger her memory. The two of us might have been in the car together or the temperature might have struck as high as it had during those late-summer days.

"Remember when we took that trip down to Virginia? We opened the windows and listened to the music. God, that was fun."

"It was," I would say, sometimes with a touch of eye-rolling reluctance.

Not that it was not fun. It was, but only to whatever degree a twelve-year-old son can have fun on a solo journey with his mother. I believe we each similarly recollected the event, not like one of those happenings in which my retelling diverged inexplicably from hers or vice versa. No, I suspected that this particular memory just might have meant somewhat more to her than to me. At least at first.

A strange reality of the illness, what the mind sheds and what the mind stores. Perhaps neurologists can explain the development based on the segments of the brain that deteriorate. In many cases, the portion that filters music sits uncorrupted. Even as those afflicted slip into the latter stages of the disease, they can recall songs. Maybe not the lyrics, but the melodies.

Fascinating to observe. You could join the person on a long, verbal rollercoaster that curls and coils in surreal directions, only for the ride to brake abruptly in stone-cold reality when hearing the initial bars of a familiar tune. Especially true for my mother, for whom music served such an important function. Gifted with a great voice, she had appeared in many stage shows and even on the radio in her youth. A modest reprieve for all of us that she did not have to hand over such a vital part of herself to the sickness.

As I expanded my personal song collection, I included a few selections specifically with her in mind, for our drives to the coffee shop and the park. I would have one cued up to begin right when we would back out of the driveway. The first few notes would startle her, happily so, as if she were the guest of honor at a surprise party, eyes flashing, a sunrise smile across her face. More than the delight of recognition. The exultant relief of having something so invaluable, something believed long lost, returned to her.

I would play "In the Cool, Cool, Cool of the Evening" or "I've Got You Under My Skin" and she would say, "I like this one." She would lift her arms like a conductor, her wrists swaying back and forth with the rhythm, even singing along at points. I also attempted to introduce a new song every so often, those with a similar style to her favorites, songs like Shirley Bassey's version of Don McLean's "And I Love You So."

"Her voice," my mother said. "Something else."

One day, she heard the recording of Frank Sinatra's "All the Way."

"I know this one."

"Yes, you do. You sang it to Dad at your engagement party."

"I did?"

"You did."

She paused for several seconds and looked out the window. Contentedly so, from appearances, her mouth twitching upward, the objects and colors streaming past her. The music seemed to break through the sensory silo of sound to become a material experienced by touch, drawn into the lungs like air. I had no idea if my mother could remember even a flash or a shadow from her performance at the engagement party, but the very possibility it had occurred placed her in the vicinity of the sublime.

"The two of us drove to Virginia once," I said.

"We did?"

"We did. We opened the windows and we played music on the radio, just like today."

"That sounds like fun."

"It was fun."

The fun, not necessarily over. The music, not necessarily of an exclusive vintage.

One afternoon, with my library set on shuffle and with Etta James' "Never My Love" coming to a close, I did not react quickly enough to skip ahead to a song I knew my mother would like. Instead, we went right into "Freddie's Dead" by Curtis Mayfield, an R&B-soul classic from the film *Super Fly*. Not exactly in line with her taste.

"Sorry about that," I said, extending my arm to jump to another track.

"Why? I like it."

"You do?"

"It's got … It's got something to it."

She squinted as if she listened through her eyes. She moved her neck along with the beat.

"He's telling a story, right?" she asked.

"He is. It's about Fat Freddie. He gets hit by a car when trying to run away from the police."

"Well, that doesn't sound good."

"He's just a character in a movie."

She was glad to hear it.

"There's a lot going on," she said. "It's different. It's interesting."

"It is. One of the best, most complex songs of its era. Any era, really."

"The 'dunh-dunh-dunh' and 'dunh-dunh-dunh' keep it together," she said, holding up her hand, as if she grabbed the handle of a mug. "But I like the … What do you call them? You can hear them behind it all?"

"The orchestra? The strings?"

"Maybe. It's a new sound, isn't it?"

When I thought my mother could impress me no further, "Freddie's Dead" reached the two-minute-and-forty-two-second mark.

"Do you hear that?" she said, sticking out her right index finger, as if pointing to the sound in the air.

"What?"

"That. There."

I paid closer attention. There it was. From two minutes and forty-two seconds to three minutes and three seconds, a soft note in the background sails like a missile overhead, crashing into the foreground.

"It's falling," she said. "And louder. Like the car sound, with the lights."

"A siren. Like a siren."

"I think so."

"You're right. I've never heard that before. I've listened to this song so many times over the years. A thousand times, maybe. I never noticed it."

Later, after taking her back to the house, I would replay the track again and again. Damn, the woman had nailed it.

"I should listen to more songs with you," I said.

She laughed. "I liked it. Any more?"

"Yes, a few more."

"Good. Let's listen."

20

"HOW LONG DOES IT TAKE?"

You unofficially graduate in the divorce process—or any transition, I imagine—when others begin to solicit your advice rather than dispense their own. You may not consider yourself ready, as if a governing body must evaluate and license you. ("Having logged the requisite number of hours in miserable contemplation and having successfully attained a state of mind in which he can review the topic without plummeting immediately into self-denigration, through the authority granted to us, we hereby deem the bearer qualified to discuss his divorce with the general public.") No, you become ready when someone senses he or she can ask a question and you decide to answer, rather than disengage with, "I don't know," or, "I'm not really ready to talk about it."

In some instances, the conversation would start by chance, like when the electrician installed a new circuit board.

"If you don't mind my asking, do you live in this place by yourself?"

"Not originally. Let's just call it my False Starter Home."

"I'm going through the same thing," he said. He opened up about his soon-to-be-ex-wife leaving him for another man, one whom he viewed so suspiciously, he fought to gain sole custody of his children. He told me about his battles with alcohol, his experimentation with drugs, anything to numb a pain he never anticipated, just enough to let him sleep for a few hours each night.

In other instances, people facilitated formal introductions to fellow travelers on Route Suddenly One. ("Could you talk to this guy from work? He's just at the start of what you're going through.") An email or a text would initiate communication, with a phone call usually to follow. The discussions would seesaw awkwardly at the beginning. I would attempt to introduce some degree of balance with humor.

"I stumbled upon a syllogism to prove the presence of a higher being: God hates me; therefore, God exists."

"I woke up each morning wearing a Washington Generals jersey." (Note: The Washington Generals have acted as the historical opponent of the Harlem Globetrotters. The Generals reportedly have lost all but three games to the Globetrotters over more than sixty years of frequent competition.)

If my new acquaintances laughed, they recognized how I understood their temporary mania. They knew I would not interpret their neuroticism as the reason for the divorce, but rather as a side effect. Not evidence of an underlying disorder, but the result of a massive destabilization. The first call often would lead to meeting for coffee or a drink. We would swap stories about sleep deprivation and paralyzing loneliness without worrying if the other person stifled cries of "Just get over it already." Organic, one-on-one support groups, without dues or a charter or the assignment of enumerated steps.

Irrespective of how the contact was made, either informally or formally, almost without fail, each of the individuals with whom I spoke posed a variation of the same question.

"How long does it take?"

Human nature, I suppose, desires objective answers to subjective questions. I certainly do. You wish to know the timeline at the outset, as if undertaking physical therapy after surgery. Subjective, though, the process stubbornly remains. Without instructions and temporal markers, you can spin yourself dizzy solely on the issue of efficacy. If you get over the divorce too quickly, are you really over it? Are you shortcutting the process, only to break down months or years later? Alternatively, if you marinate too long, does the divorce blend with your identity? Do you risk having others say, "He's still getting over it," even though no one else remembers the marriage in the first place, since so many years have passed? Your epitaph would read: *Cadent a latere semper repudium*—Always consumed by divorce.

When it came to pace, I confess to some rather critical observations regarding the freshly separated. Those who had torn their lives down to the studs and refashioned a shiny edifice seemingly overnight. Those who strolled hand-in-hand with a new companion without having completed the paperwork to let go of the previous partner. I would think: *That was quick.* Those whom I judged could have, quite rightly, replied, "It's none of you damn business." In truth, one's relationship with time during this period might be the most personal, the most private. This reality, divorce rookies have yet to grasp. So, the topic of time almost always arose. Like with that one woman.

Early in August, I attended an outdoor concert organized by my town, the type of deliberate civic programming with a looks-like, feels-like sense of community I unashamedly enjoy. I invited a few friends. They were fans of the band, one that years ago had abandoned recording its own music to throw itself proudly and profitably into covering the greatest hits of artists in the pop-rock pantheon. Searching for seats, we navigated our way through the crowd of pre-teens, older adults and young families. I overheard one early-thirties mother say as she bounced in place with an infant in her arms, "I used to go to the free concerts in Bryant Park all the time. I have to settle for this, I guess." From the evening trains dribbled fathers with rolled-sleeves and loosened ties, who—perhaps conscious of onlookers—kissed their wives on the forehead and high-fived their children in a somewhat unnatural demonstration of domestic elation. My friends and I located a spot toward the back of the green. Blankets down, I volunteered to get pizza from one of the nearby trucks. As I waited, the group began its rendition of "Brandy (You're a Fine Girl)."

"I love this song," said the woman in front of me to her husband. "I never can remember the band."

"Beats me," he answered.

"Looking Glass," I said, trying to lend neighborly assistance, but quite possibly sounding like a know-it-all.

"Book this guy on *Jeopardy*," the husband said. Confirmed: I sounded like a know-it-all.

Another woman—one right behind me, close to my age, with brown hair, pleading hazel eyes and the complexion of a marshmallow browned over a campfire—spoke only so I could hear her. "The drummer from Looking Glass was in the band that played at my wedding."

"Really? That's interesting," I said.

"I hate thinking about it now. It still doesn't seem possible we are getting divorced."

"I am sorry to hear that." She did not wish for the exchange to conclude on that point. I knew, since I would not have wished for the exchange to conclude had I introduced the same subject, in a similar manner, to a complete stranger, months earlier. "I understand."

"You do? How long has it been? I'm just getting started."

Without giving me the chance to respond, she dumped all over the grass every article of the couple's dirty laundry. They had stopped talking. Separate vacations. No holidays with each other's family. No physical intimacy for what seemed like years. This last point compelled me to intervene, as if she were a lost tourist who held up a map in a dangerous section of a city.

"I don't mean to be rude, but you really shouldn't be sharing this information with someone you just met."

"I'm sorry. I've lost my filter."

"I get it. I did the same."

"I'm going to think about this conversation later and regret it, aren't I?"

"We'll give you a Mulligan."

"Mulligan?"

"It's a golf term. It means we won't count that stroke."

"Golf, uggghhh ... Do you play? My husband played way too much." She caught herself. "I'm doing it again, aren't I?"

"It's fine. And, no, I don't play golf, but I've taken my fair share of Mulligans."

"You seem to be doing well now."

"I'm glad I seem to be doing well."

"Uggghhh, don't say that." (She liked to make the "uggghhh" sound.) "If you aren't any better, I don't have hope."

"I'm fine now. Really, I am. You will be, too."

She slanted her head and tightened her mouth into a thin, skeptical smile. "Should I believe someone I just met when he tells me I will be fine? What did you think when strangers told you you would be fine?"

"Fair enough. No, I didn't believe them, but that doesn't mean they weren't right. I'm fine."

"How long does it take?"

We had arrived.

Since she had prodded me a bit, I considered challenging her. What does "it" even mean? Not thinking about the divorce every minute of every hour? Moving on with another person? Accepting the advantages and disadvantages of a singular lifestyle? Waiting for pizza without unadvisedly baring your soul to the unknown individual ahead of you? The probing of a didactic jerk, no doubt. Not what she needed. Not what I would have needed in her position. I also empathized with her subtext: *Will it be too late for me?* I decided to reply gently, if vaguely.

"People are different."

"Really?" she said, cramming immense incredulity into only six letters, not having to add, "That's the best you can do?"

"It just takes time."

You learn some clichés become clichés, not only because they are succinct and accessible, but because they impart truth. "It just takes time" relayed a good deal of truth. Almost everyone who suffers an emotional setback eventually lands on the same line, at the same pharmacy, waiting for the same prescription: time. You might, at first, despise the static properties, hoping for the many somber hours to speed by and the fewer fun minutes to slow down. Begrudgingly, you realize time's relentlessness gives you what you otherwise lack: certainty. The days do not wait. Time does not care about you. The indifference somehow heals. Your personal adversity shrinks in the distance. Your myopia broadens. Your preoccupations expose themselves as insignificant.

The woman's eyes opened more widely. She desired color beyond "It just takes time." She wanted the thunderbolt. She wanted to hear how I had climbed to Machu Picchu and drenched the Peruvian soil with my tears, only for a magnificent tree to have sprung up instantly on site, bearing fruit for future generations of heartbroken divorcees. She wanted to hear about a coffee shop meet-cute, in which an eligible Myrna Loy clone and I grabbed the same drink, thus sparking playful repartee that blazed into full-on romance. She wanted to hear how she would get up one morning and feel as if everything was all right. She wanted to hear how such a morning could come as early as tomorrow.

Not how it worked. Not for me, at least. I could tell her only of the boring, seemingly wasted days. The twenty-four-hour segments absolutely identical to their predecessors and successors. Up in the morning, off to work, back to bed. Only in stringing enough of them together did the quantity prove invaluable. One after the other after the other.

The woman's persistence forced me to define and describe my methods extemporaneously, clumsily so.

"Look, at every step, I would tell myself I was fine. Even the first day, when everything shattered, I would insist I was fine. I believed it, too. But three months later, I would look back and I had to admit how wrong I was. I wasn't fine, not compared to how I felt right then. And three months after that, I did the same thing. I looked back and saw I was wrong. I kept doing this. Only when I could think of a day three months earlier and honestly say I was fine at that time, I knew I had made real progress."

"That's a little confusing," she said.

"You don't make things easy."

"That's what my husband would say."

"I'm sorry. I still don't like hearing other people repeat my wife's criticism, even when I know it's accurate. Especially when I know it's accurate."

"You said wife, not ex-wife. You need another three months."

"How about this?" I said. "You will remember this day one year from now. When you do, you will appreciate how far you have come."

"That's it?"

"That's the best I can do right now."

"I'll find you in three months and see if you can do better," she said.

I made it to the counter and gathered the pizza. My hands full, I nodded and left, my quick departure blamed on the unspoken excuse of having to clear out for the next customers. Not much more I could have done for her. I located my friends and sat on the blanket beside them. Bug spray wafted in the night air. The band began to play "Gimme Shelter," an edgy selection for the crowd, with a chorus punctuated by cries of "rape" and "murder." I bit into my dinner and, of course, thought of that woman. I might have expected to say to myself, *Glad I'm not her*, or, more precisely, *Glad I'm no longer her*. Yet I almost envied her, a rather twisted, mystifying admission.

Even now, not too far removed from my most difficult days, I reminisce with a peculiar fondness. Those moments, the most despairing, I recall with a remember-when nostalgia reserved for high school or family vacations. I think of those mornings on the park bench, staring jealously at the ducks floating in the brook. I remember sitting in my car, in the parking lot of the grocery store on a Thursday night, with nowhere else to go. In bed at three in the morning, in that transitional hour, despondent over what had come before and so anxious over what would follow. For whatever reason, I sometimes miss those days. Perhaps a life in crisis feels a bit more real.

In the nighttime breeze, parents wrapped their children in sweatshirts, which made me wish someone would do the same to me. The band introduced its final song. I wondered to myself: *Am I really as far along as I would like to think? As that woman seemed to believe?* Maybe not. After all, with some regularity, I still experienced an unusual phenomenon. I would doze off for only a few minutes on the train in the morning or in the evening. I would awake suddenly, my neck snapping up, a single thought rocketing through my head, as if inhaled into my skull through my nose and mouth at once: *I am divorced.* Like a machine resetting itself, my mind would return to the beginning, then race through the years, past my youth, past my marriage, into a baffling present. Again: *I am divorced.* I would look around to see if anyone had noticed. Not quite the behavior of a person completely over anything.

The concert finished, I walked my friends to their cars, then returned to my house. The easy sweep of the front door. The footstep thuds that expanded the entryway into a cavern. The silence that greeted me. All reminded me of those first days when I began to live alone. I just stood there for a few minutes, listening to the appliances buzz and the floors settle. So many hours spent within those creaking walls. For all of my laconic platitudes about conceding to the ruthlessness of time, I still wished I could control it somehow.

What if, just once, I could have disrupted the unyielding flow of minutes and years? More than disrupt, what if I could have gone back? At what instant would I have entered? What event might I have altered? Would I have pinpointed the exact second my marriage had transitioned from critical to terminal, as if I ever could have begun to guess when that might have taken place? Would I have reversed the circumstances that had set the divorce in motion?

No.

I wished only to return to one period. I would visit my slightly younger self, the one so lost in the first days and weeks and months of his divorce. The one so convinced all of his choices had funneled to ruination. The one who employed only the darkest superlatives: worst, hardest, strangest, loneliest, emptiest.

I would say to that person: "You cannot believe what I will tell you at this minute, but please trust me. You will be fine. Better than fine. I have seen the future. You will have a lot of difficult days, but none you cannot get through, perhaps to your surprise. Your life may not be better. It may not be worse. It will be different and you will appreciate those differences. And you would not trade it for anything. I promise you."

21

"DO I KNOW YOUR MOTHER?"

"Actually, you are my mother."

"I am?"

"You are."

"I didn't know that. How long have I been your mother?"

"For as long as I can remember."

"That's amazing. Really?"

"Really."

22

THE MINUTES TICKED BY as I sat in Saint Anne's. I filed away a few details from the surroundings, specifics that would have authenticated whatever description I ordinarily would have brought home. ("I sat right near 'this.'" "I saw 'that.'") Pointless, though. Only my mother would have cared. For her, the word "Quebec" had vaporized on impact during our phone call on the drive from the airport the prior night. Pointless.

Over the months, I had come to understand my mother and I faced a similar problem, although from radically different angles: memory. I wanted to forget. She wanted to remember. Quite the contrast, that as my mother strained to hold on to her memories, I attempted to push mine away with equal intensity.

To draw the faintest equivalence between our states—even with a dotted line—jolts me as exploitive. My memory, I could live with, while hers had become increasingly difficult to live without. What does it matter if I felt a pang during a holiday when my mother could forget to consume enough liquid to maintain a healthy hydration level?

In listening to each of us, you could hear how we employed opposite techniques to manage the same challenge. I stripped down my memories. I consciously shifted to the singular pronoun, as in, "I once went there," and, "I moved into the house," hopeful that language could reprogram me. My retellings became less personal, less textured, just hulking monoliths of time. I began to sound like a person with something to hide, as if I had stolen a drifter's identity or embezzled funds from an Angolan oil company. My mother, on the other hand, would scoop up loose fragments and assemble them into a semi-coherent remembrance. Her head, a giant box of Legos emptied onto a playroom floor. She would snap together pieces of various colors and sizes with no regard for cohesion, the final product a beautifully misshapen art project. I had to applaud the woman. She retained her talent with language, her sentences like excerpts from a draft of *Finnegans Wake*.

"We've been to that place before. Chuttles. Up on the hill, that really big, magnificent building with the fun ladies and the songs. Maxy was there, too. Sometimes. He was so … What was he? Crankity. Did you know him? He always said things, like, 'Now, remember what I told you about going there.' And I laughed. It was nice."

Perhaps due to our methods, more and more detached from our memories my mother and I became. I began to feel as though I remembered someone else's life. I could recall going places and seeing things, but more so as a spectator than a participant. Perhaps my mother experienced the inverse. She might have felt as if she were leading a life she could not remember. Maybe she awakened each day questioning how she had arrived in that bed, why she was in that house among those people. Neither of us could make sense of our pasts, which left us both uneasy in our presents.

The more and more detached from our memories, the more and more detached from ourselves we became. At least I thought as much. The line dividing person from memory invariably blurs, if one could pencil in such a line in the first place. All we have accomplished. All we have weathered. Our character. Our personality. Everything housed in memory. The disease only reinforces this construct, with the consistent refrain, "We are losing her." Are we still ourselves if we do not remember who we were? Are we still ourselves if we do not wish to remember who we were? The questions, while perhaps relevant, read like showy, inflated opening lines from some first-year instructor during an intro-to-whatever course in college. Regardless, I did not know the answers.

My mother and I did not raise such ideas with one another during our drives to the coffee shop or on our walks around the lake in the park. We could not.

"What do I do with the memories?" I might have asked her, if she had maintained her faculties. At one time, she would have given a good answer, I suspect. A poetic one, stunning and soulful, grounded in affection and wrapped with enough mystery to force my head to work a little to figure it out. She would trace the outline within which I would have to color.

"What do I do without the memories?" she might have asked me, if she could articulate the winnowing of her cognition. I would have given an unsatisfactory answer, I suspect. I would have gulped and choked on the hard sadness. Powerless before such a question, I probably would have said rather weakly, "Who knows?"

This conversation we could not have with one another still very much there between us. I would return her to the house and move on with my day until seeing her next. She would struggle. We would meet again, puzzled and discouraged, but unable to describe to the other exactly why.

Unexpectedly, as my mother's illness worsened, an answer to the questions might have emerged. In no way do I wish to offer a sunny-side interpretation of an atrocious assault, a daily theft of the individual's most precious item: the self kept from view of everyone, the self no one sees. Nor do I wish to present her solely as a utility to aid my personal development. Yet as my mother suffered so excruciatingly, she unknowingly taught me another lesson.

"We are losing her."

No, not quite.

The more time we spent with one another, the farther away her past had slipped, I began to resent such a statement. To claim we had lost my mother due to her failing memory would reduce her simply to memories. She was more than everything that came before her. She was more than what would follow. She could not recall scripts she had written or trips she had taken or the students she had taught. Did this reduction leave her less of a person? Less of my mother? Did her days amount to less because she no longer could call them up from her archive? No, not at all.

Not only the positive faded away, I could not help but notice. My mother no longer could remember the many occasions I had disappointed her, the profound frustrations I had visited upon her daily. That is, after all, what sons do to mothers. I no longer could remember the many occasions she had driven me mad, the irrational expectations she had visited upon me daily. That is, after all, what mothers do to sons.

What remained? Something not fully contained within neurological barriers. A moment not reliant on the past, nor validated by the future. All of which might have appeared incomprehensible to the outside world. Perhaps on one of our outings, someone might have seen us and asked, "Remember what she was like?"

I would have replied, "This is who she is now."

Not to discard completely the memories. One day, when my mother passes, I no doubt will retreat into remembrances of her. I will edit out the labored breaths taken during her final hours, the tubes, the dried blood on the tape wrapped around the needles in failing veins. I will focus on that morning when I was four years old and announced that I would run away from home. My mother packed my bag, then hers, and the two of us spent a few hours in the backyard, until I had changed my mind and asked if we could return. I will run through the many late nights in high school, when she had stayed up with me to review and correct my essays.

Not to say the memories no longer mattered to her, even as the disease advanced. Actually, perhaps because the disease had advanced. At one point, bringing attention to the past seemed as gratuitous as administering CPR on a body already declared deceased. When my mother had retained just enough to understand how much she had forgotten, that tip-of-the-tongue, hand-clamped aggravation of trying to recall a trivial fact radiated through every second of her day. Then, when she at last had relinquished even the urge to remember, no more hostility. No longer a loss, since she could not recall the possession.

"You know, you directed many shows. Dozens, if not over a hundred. You were a playwright, too. You wrote several plays. You earned a graduate degree in theater."

"I did?"

"You did."

"That's amazing. I never knew that."

"You were a superb teacher. Your students are all grown adults and they still talk about how much you influenced their lives."

"Really?"

"Yes. And you were a fantastic athlete, too. You loved basketball. Even in your mid-fifties, you could sink eight-out-of-ten free throws."

"I could? I didn't know that."

Appreciation for the experiences ever having taken place, even if she could not picture the images or recreate the setting or recapture the mood. Memories perhaps matter less than assumed.

As I sat in the basilica outside of Quebec City, maybe not so pointless. When I returned home, I would tell my mother of the visit. We would get in the car and I would explain how she had driven to Quebec over the years, how I had decided to follow her example, how I went looking for the same guidance she had sought.

"That sounds terrific. I didn't know I did that."

"You did. You did many things that were terrific."

"I did?"

"You did."

We then would sit in the coffee shop. She would drink her green tea latte and say, "This is so good."

She would observe the customers walking in and say, "Isn't this fun?"

She would exist in that moment, the one she would forget almost as soon as it had occurred. The next day, my mother might not recall my name, perhaps never to do so again. She might have forgotten on a Friday that she had cared for me on a Tuesday. Did her care mean any less when she expressed it? No, not at all. True to her in the moment. No less true when the moment had passed, remembered or not.

"What do I do with the memories?" I might have asked her.

She might have answered, "Live with them. Live without them."

23

I WANTED IT TO END.

Not my life. Never had I wrestled with the self-destructive, fortunately for me. Family members and friends later would admit to their worry over my potential to harm myself. I should have clued in on this concern when they would keep me on the phone a little longer than usual some evenings, when they would drop in at my house without much warning, just to say hello. The most startling—and most thoughtful—example occurred when my brother's father-in-law called him after my niece's birthday party, having overheard me joke about how easily someone could clear out my home if I ever suddenly passed away. (I believe culling possessions demonstrates one's healthy acknowledgment of personal mortality.) My brother reported having to mollify for nearly an hour his father-in-law, who insisted that everyone should listen seriously to my cry for help. He and those around me truly had no reason to fear. If nothing else, I maintained an overflowing reserve of spite to fuel me.

I only wished for this period to end. I had put in the hard work, so I thought. I had logged the hours on my own. Walked miles and miles. Avoided the shortcuts. Steered away from anger and toward acceptance. Set aside the artificial, meaningless schedule by which to substantiate my life, the one in which I would have achieved "X" by a certain age, accomplished "Y" by another. I cared about the unimportant less and the important more. I had trained myself to value the simplicity and nuance I previously would have raced past on my way to the next destination.

I had done all of it, yet still felt so ... Afflicted? Tentative? Incomplete? Detached? Maybe bored? Just not myself. Or worse. What if I had become fully, completely the next variant of myself—the post-divorce self—and this state of being represented the best I could muster?

I had dispensed with expectations regarding enlightenment, with the fallacy that wisdom would shine through in a single instant. The closest I had come to an epiphany? The embrace of my own inconsequence, a truth accepted little-by-little over an extended duration.

I do not matter.

To those who cared about me, yes, I mattered, but not in any grander scheme. Did the world stall its rotation as it awaited an answer as to whether or not a male in his late-thirties would find happiness? Of course not. Will he trust again? Will he scrounge up a sufficient reason to get up each day? No one cares. People go on living. Bills need paying. Illnesses need healing. All of which says nothing of the farther-reaching crises besieging humanity.

Again, I do not matter.

No disappointment with this embrace of my inconsequence. Only relief. The lower the stakes, the lighter the load. When the needle does not even quiver due to an outcome, the intensity subsides. Unattainable goals—contentment, balance, buying a greeting card, cleaning out a garage—become attainable. Yet even with my more reasonable perspective, the constant self-absorption had drained me dry. I had grown so tired of having to prop up my moods, of having to carry through every day a body so tight and tense.

Not just for myself did I want it to end. I no longer wished to trouble others. I had taken up enough of everyone's time. I wanted my father to feel optimism, not just temporary satisfaction with my ability to gut out a rough period. I wanted my mother to process images of me happy and secure, so she perhaps could sleep through the night.

What more did I need to do?

On a Saturday morning in October, I finished my errands earlier than usual. Dry cleaners. Bank. Hardware store for a new rake. I returned to my home and climbed the stairs to the room on the third floor. I would head there when I sought total solitude, which made absolutely no sense, since I lived by myself and people rarely looked for me. I had kept the area mostly clear, except for an ironing board. The space held unrealized potential: the bedroom for the child that did not come to be. When first touring the house and later moving in—without voicing our plans—we had designated the third floor as the eventual nursery. Maybe only I did, in retrospect. No furniture went there. Unlike every other room, we did not paint, but left it the neutral color recommended to sellers by realtors. One day, some shade of blue or pink or sage green would have covered the walls. A crib with far-too-complicated assembly instructions would have followed. Then, stuffed animals and mobiles and a monitor gifted by a friend who would declare the device indispensible. "One day" never arrived.

Now, just a quiet, deserted, open floor at the top of a dwelling a bit too large for one person. I could lie flat on my back on the carpet, my arms extended out. I listened to cars whoosh by outside, mimicking the soothing sound of rushing water. Staring up at the ceiling at the rather drab, serviceable light fixture, I considered shopping for a more stylish one that afternoon. I would have something to show for my weekend. What else? Another movie that evening? The quality of the films had started to improve as Oscar season approached, but still not so appealing. Would the weather be warm enough for me to sit on the park bench by the brook the next morning?

What am I doing?

I exhaled exasperation and self-disgust, saliva trailing at the end, which kicked up coughs and gags as it fell into my throat. My entire self contracted into that trope that defines insanity as repeating the same action and expecting a different result. I wanted it to end, but what would change after another movie, another hike? Nothing. Not to discount those measures. They worked—until they did not.

Intervention. I needed a self-guided intervention, which sounded dreadfully clinical and not exactly in line with my plight. Intervention more as a break in the routine, rather than as an antidote to an addiction. Something beyond myself.

Why not?

Crazy ideas puff like bubbles through plastic rings dipped in bottles of opalescent solution. They form, float, shimmer and pop in only seconds. Sometimes, one bubble outlives the others, lifting higher, holding together, demanding attention. The crazy idea I had on that Saturday morning on the third floor of my house kept lifting, kept holding, kept demanding.

Why not? Nothing to lose. Something different.

I weighed the pros and cons. Reviewed my calendar. No conflicts. Nothing stopping me, other than what typically stopped me: myself. I sat up, wrapped my arms around my bent knees for another minute or two. I stood. I had a flight to book and a hotel to reserve and a bag to pack.

24

ONLY EIGHT MINUTES until the bus driver would exit the parking lot. Still seated, my tired eyes melding the rows of ivory arches into a mass, I breathed in deeply, the air the sound of a crashing wave inside my head. I hesitated a few seconds. Then, a few more. I irrationally waited to see if something might happen, that if I departed one beat too early, I just might have missed the payoff, like the time I had skipped out in the eighth inning of a seemingly lost game in the World Series, only for my team to have staged an epic comeback. ("You left Saint Anne's too soon! One more minute and you would have been there for the rapture!")

The simple act of standing became the rubber-meets-the-road contest between pragmatism and faith. The internal opposition pinned me to the pew. As much as I had drilled realism—and, yes, cynicism—into my head, a small part of me—an embarrassing part—held out hope for some sort of hocus-pocus transformation. Regardless of whatever interior battle I waged, the bus still would head back to the city. Drivers with schedules to keep do not wait for the resolution of metaphysical-existential questions. Quite a comforting reality, I had come to realize. One often requires a bit of life to pull you back into living. I stood.

Rather than walk down the center aisle up which I had entered, I turned left toward the perimeter. Against the wall, I found an assemblage of candles, the tiers of red and green and blue and cream votives. In the Catholic tradition, one lights a candle in a church to offer an intention, perhaps to aid a sick friend or to get direction during a personal crisis. Even lax adherents to the religion partake in the ritual, as if holding on to one last memento from a failed relationship. I probably had slipped into the category of "lax adherent."

As most churches do, the basilica suggested a donation for each candle, a not-unreasonable *quid pro quo*. My shoulders dropped, the corners of my mouth flexed, my eye slowly closed. I had nothing on me. I reviewed, with reproach, the various points I could have visited a bank since I had landed in Quebec. There might have been an ATM at the candy store. There definitely had to be one by the tourism center. Perhaps I would have had time to withdraw money in the airport if that immigration agent had not taken me aside.

"You've been here before?"

"No."

"Your passport says you were in Canada several years ago, no?"

"I thought you meant Quebec. Yes, I have been to Canada."

I had been to Canada.

On my honeymoon.

With this realization came a physical awareness of the properties that move and govern the world. Time. Gravity. Air. Light. Slow and heavy and cold and bright, the surroundings pulsed against me, through me.

I did carry Canadian currency, which I had kept with me for over a decade.

At the conclusion of a one-week honeymoon spent in a western province, a small amount of cash remained. Rather than exchange the two Canadian ten-dollar bills, I had placed them in my wallet, where they would rest for years and years. When I would conduct any number of simple transactions over the course of a day, I would see a private, personal reminder of my marriage. The ring, the certificates, everything else, just symbols and signifiers for the public and the state. All somewhat easily removed and discarded in the division. Not that money, about which I either had forgotten entirely or to which I unconsciously had clung.

My sternum popped with a quick laugh. I shook my head, as if to acknowledge to whoever or whatever had orchestrated the moment: *I get it.* I removed the bills, folded them and stuck them halfway into the slot of the donation bin. I paused. A lie to claim it was easy to let go. I shoved them forward, my palm pressed hard against the cold metal, a piece of me falling into the chamber.

I then lit two candles.

One, for my parents. For my mother, who would continue to decline, who could not make a final visit to Sainte-Anne-de-Beaupré. For my father, who would sacrifice himself in her care, who would suffer and lose so much more than the rest of us.

Please give them strength. Please let them know they are loved.

One, for all those who had supported me throughout my challenges. The family and friends who did not allow me to feel alone for one minute. That they never would doubt their significance in the world.

Please give them strength. Please let them know they are loved.

I backed away from the candles. With a ride still to catch, my body went toward the door as if submerged in water, partly floating, partly slogging. Of course, I could not let what had just taken place simply be. No, I had to analyze it right then. Even a quasi-marvel can alter one's personality only so much.

Had I foisted meaning onto an otherwise ordinary convergence of unrelated factors? Probably, but I already had subscribed to something beyond myself by carrying the money in the first place, by flying to Quebec, by waiting in that church for over thirty minutes. I could read into that instant several interpretations.

My mother had granted me a gift, a lifetime of devotion and love captured in a message she no longer could deliver.

Saint Anne had nudged me to move if not in a new direction, at the very least onward, as she had my mother decades earlier.

The universe had reminded me that after I had accepted disenchantment, some type of magic remains, even if only in the form of coincidence.

Perhaps I simply had neglected to withdraw Canadian currency.

I do not know for certain. I never will. Does it matter?

Outside, I reached the bus. Before grabbing the railing and taking that first step to board, I looked back at the basilica.

In my mind, Saint Anne had given the answer.

CPSIA information can be obtained
at www.ICGtesting.com
Printed in the USA
BVHW032222250620
582362BV00001B/99